B55 070 997 7

SW1

ROTHERHAM LIBRARIES AND NEIGHBOURHOOD HUBS

D0726900

FUTURE ALEX NOBODY

The
a fu

KATE GILBY SMITH

ORION CHILDREN'S BOOKS

First published in Great Britain in 2021 by Hodder & Stoughton

1 3 5 7 9 10 8 6 4 2

Text copyright © Kate Gilby Smith, 2020
Illustrations copyright © Thy Bui, 2020

The moral rights of the author and illustrator have been asserted.

All characters and events in this publication, other than those clearly
in the public domain, are fictitious and any resemblance to
real persons, living or dead, is purely coincidental.

In order to create a sense of setting, some names of real places have been
included in the book. However, the events depicted in this book are imaginary
and the real places used fictitiously.

All rights reserved.
No part of this publication may be reproduced, stored in
a retrieval system, or transmitted, in any form or by any means, without
the prior permission in writing of the publisher, nor be otherwise circulated
in any form of binding or cover other than that in which it is published
and without a similar condition including this condition being
imposed on the subsequent purchaser.

A CIP catalogue record for this book
is available from the British Library.

ISBN 978 1 51010 837 0

Printed and bound in Great Britain by Clays Ltd, Elcograf S.p.A.

The paper and board used in this book are made
from wood from responsible sources.

Orion Children's Books
An imprint of
Hachette Children's Group
Part of Hodder & Stoughton
Carmelite House
50 Victoria Embankment
London EC4Y 0DZ

An Hachette UK Company

www.hachette.co.uk
www.hachettechildrens.co.uk

For my parents,
Chris and Robin

CONTENTS

CHAPTER ONE

Tourists at the Hospital

On the night she was born, there were thirty-two newborns in the maternity ward, tiny things with screwed up, angry faces screaming together in a chorus. This made life extremely difficult for a man called Henry, who was squinting through thick glasses over a sea of pink and blue hats. Somewhere among the thirty-two cradles lay his baby niece, but no matter how hard he looked, he couldn't work out which one she was.

This wasn't a great start for his new role as an uncle. But you could forgive Henry, considering what had already happened that evening. A call had come in from the hospital just as he was taking a meal-for-one out of the oven, when a softly spoken nurse told him that his dear sister had gone into labour.

On his arrival at the hospital, having run the whole way there in his socks, Henry had to dodge a white double-decker coach pulling up at the entrance. A long line of men, women and children unloaded from the coach and traipsed noisily through the hospital doors. Henry barely noticed the commotion. Had he taken a moment to look, he might have seen that there was something rather peculiar about the people piling past him into reception. One man with a very long nose was dressed for camping, complete with walking boots and a compass hanging around his neck. There was a woman nearby wearing a yellow straw hat, so wide that it tickled people's noses whenever she turned her head. A teenage boy was struggling under a rucksack large enough to fit a mid-sized bear inside.

As it happened, Henry didn't notice any of this; despite his unusually big brain, he had never been known for his powers of observation. He pushed through the crowd (or, to be more accurate, the crowd pushed him) and found a map of the hospital. As he studied the route to the maternity ward, more and more people piled into the cramped reception area, until it was so loud he could barely hear himself think. He caught a few phrases, like 'Come on, quickly!' and

'It's almost time!', and wished that the speakers would kindly lower their voices. Though he wouldn't have dreamed of complaining, disapproval must have been written across his face because the woman with the yellow hat gawped at him as he passed by.

At the ward, a nurse took Henry to a small room with hard chairs and a thirsty-looking fern. A doctor came, an older woman with very kind, watery eyes. She sat Henry down, put an arm around his shoulder, and told him that there had been complications with the birth. His sister had passed away. The baby's father had left the picture months before. And so the newborn entered the world very much alone.

This was how Henry found himself, shivering, tears sliding down the bridge of his nose, in a room full of crying babies. He'd never liked babies much; they put him on edge, so fragile looking that even one glance might break them. But now, he thought, their wails echoing like a drill around his skull, they were more likely to break him.

When eventually he found the right crib, Henry knew for certain it was his niece, not because he recognised his sister in her features, or indeed because there was anything special about the way she looked; she was a baby like any other. He knew it was her because she was the only one without a name tag. Peering down into the baby's shocked brown eyes, Henry had a strange feeling that he'd been waiting for this moment all his life.

CHAPTER TWO

The Birthday Party

Thinking of a name for the baby proved to be one of the easiest jobs Henry had in the first few weeks of being an uncle. He bought a book of baby names and flicked through the pages. He didn't need to go very far before he was satisfied; in fact, he went no further than the As.

'Alex, Alex, Alex.' He repeated the name as he cradled the baby in his arms. 'That's a strong name, a warrior's name, don't you think?'

The baby stared up at her uncle. There was a hint of doubt in her expression as she took in Henry's plump face and thinning circle of hair.

It was no coincidence that Alex was also the name of a character in Henry's favourite computer game. In fact, he had spent most of his forty-one years with a joystick in hand, a hobby which had left his skin pale and his waist size larger than most. Working as an IT consultant, he was indoors most days, tapping away at the keyboard in his living room. Whenever he did venture out his front door, he often ended up wondering why people couldn't behave more like computers.

With his niece at home, however, there was considerably less time for playing games. Once or twice Henry tried gaming with the baby balanced on one hand, the controller in the other, but she didn't seem to like that much. So instead, he started telling Alex all about his work, technical things like *processing speeds* and *data analysis,* phrases which usually made people's eyes glaze over. To his amazement, the baby listened, watching carefully as if his every word was a rare gem and gurgling appreciatively in all the right places.

As his niece grew older, so did her curiosity about the world. 'Uncle Henry,' she would begin, her brow furrowed, a clear sign that a difficult question was about to follow. 'How does the phone work?'

'Good question, Alex,' he'd reply, excitedly. 'I've absolutely no idea! But I always find the best way to see how something works is to take it apart. Shall we?'

Then the phone – or the laptop, or the toaster, or the kettle, or the television – would be opened up, piece by piece, the pair of them huddled over it like a couple of surgeons looking for a ruptured appendix.

It wasn't long before Uncle Henry realised that his niece was not only curious – as most children are – but also had an uncommon, unrelenting drive to answer every *how* and *why* and *what* the world had to offer. By the time she was four years old, she'd completed an in-depth field study of earthworm activity in the garden. At six, she could explain – with diagrams – what keeps an aeroplane in the air. And by the time she was eight, Alex frequently beat Uncle Henry at their favourite television quiz show (the really hard one meant for university boffins). Even better than that, Alex wasn't the type of child who liked simply to be told the answer to questions; no, thank you. Alex was only content if she could work things out for herself. It was a quality that would terrify most parents. But it made Uncle Henry feel like he'd won the lottery. (Not that playing the lottery was something Uncle Henry would ever do; he knew the statistical probability of winning the jackpot was *far* too tiny.)

For a long time, their life together was gloriously simple. Uncle Henry educated Alex at home. He'd had a difficult time at school himself, which led him to believe they were places best avoided wherever possible.

As a result, the pair rarely left the safety of their small house, except when it was unavoidably necessary, like to visit the dentist or buy supplies at the local supermarket. They made fortnightly shopping trips, which in their opinion was two weeks too often. For one thing, they disliked the abundance of options. Does anyone really need seventeen varieties of mayonnaise? And for another, there were the shoppers themselves. Why did walking behind a trolley make people act even more bizarrely than normal? Uncle Henry – who could daydream through a volcano eruption – didn't always notice the odd behaviour of his fellow shoppers. But his young niece did. She noticed the woman browsing the freezer section who waved at her as if they were long lost friends. The people crouching behind cabbage crates who ducked as soon as she spotted them. Then there was the time that a complete stranger asked for her autograph while her uncle was busy choosing washing powder. And the elderly man who leapfrogged over a pyramid display of mushroom soup just to shake her hand.

Alex noticed all of these things and yet, not knowing any differently, put them down to living in a small town (which gives people licence to be a little eccentric) and to having one of those familiar kinds of faces. It was the same excuse she used the time a crowd of strangers had seemed to follow her down the street, stopping whenever she stopped and turning whenever she turned. And the time a girl she'd never seen before almost knocked her down with a running-jump-hug, shouting 'It's you, it's really you!', before being hurried away by a worried-looking adult. Her uncle – who could find a logical explanation for almost anything – chalked it up to a case of mistaken identity. But things like that happened so regularly as she grew up that Alex started to wonder if she had an identical twin.

For Uncle Henry, these occurrences provided yet more evidence that *other people* were mysterious creatures who acted in inexplicable ways. Much better to avoid social interaction wherever possible, he determined. That is why he felt particularly alarmed when, at eleven years old, Alex asked if she could attend the local school.

'I love learning from you, Uncle Henry, I really do,' she said. 'But I'd quite like to meet some children my own age.'

Alex had read all about the world in her uncle's books. She'd seen wonderful pictures of rainforests and oceans, sprawling deserts and icy glaciers. She could tell you what it would be like to live on Mars (very cold) and the number of moons circling around Saturn (eighty-two at last count). Alex had learned all of this without needing to leave her house. But now she was dying to see the universe for herself, and most of all, find some friends to share it with.

Uncle Henry was surprised. He didn't understand why she would want the company of *children her own age*, who drooled and sniffed and couldn't work out even the simplest calculus. But when he saw the hopeful look on her face he agreed at once.

By then, Alex already knew how to jump-start a car, rewire a radio and build a working bedside lamp from scratch. She could draw a map of the Milky Way entirely from memory. Henry told her new head teacher, Mrs Wright, all about this when they met on her first day, his eyes sparkling and chest puffed up with pride. But the woman didn't seem to care much. She was more concerned about what Alex was wearing – a very baggy, bottle green T-shirt which had once belonged to Henry and featured the logo of his favourite superhero film.

'I suggest,' Mrs Wright said, the nostrils of her beak-like nose flaring, 'that you take her to buy a *regulation uniform* this very afternoon.' Her eyes narrowed as she looked at Alex, who was wearing her hair as she always did, half tied up in a sprout on top of her head, the other half hanging loose to her shoulders. 'And will your hairstyle please make up its mind!' Mrs Wright added.

Fortunately, the meeting soon ended with a call from Mrs Wright's secretary reporting that a double-decker coach was blocking the school gates, along with a number of people hanging around dressed, unseasonably, for a summer holiday.

An uneasy feeling crept over Alex. She didn't know why, but somehow whenever strange things happened in her life, a double-decker coach was never far away.

'How peculiar,' said Mrs Wright, her lips a thin line. 'Why on earth would a tourist coach stop in Murford? They must have got very lost, indeed.'

Then she ushered Alex out of the door, forgetting all about the issue of her inappropriate outfit. Alex was pleased to escape her office, which had been too hot and smelled strongly of lavender. She hugged Henry – who dabbed at his eyes and mumbled something about time passing too quickly – and skipped off down the hallway after Mrs Wright to join her class.

The first lesson of the day was maths, which happened to be Alex's favourite subject. Her teacher was startled to learn that she already knew trigonometry and quadratic equations. 'My goodness,' he said, after Alex completed a particularly mind-boggling piece of mental arithmetic. 'Who taught you to do that?'

'My uncle, sir. He says that with a good grasp of mathematics there's nothing you can't do. Some people have used numbers to reach the moon.'

A couple of boys sitting at the back of the class sniggered. The larger one whispered something to the other behind his hand, and they both collapsed in a fit of laughter.

'Well!' Her teacher loosened his tie as if his neck had suddenly swelled. 'I quite agree with your uncle about that! But we're not supposed to study quadratic equations for another three years. We have a syllabus to follow, you know.'

Alex soon realised that not everything Uncle Henry had taught her was welcome at school. This became apparent at her first breaktime when she decided to take apart a brand-new school computer.

'I've never seen a computer like this before,' she explained, sitting on the floor with a mess of cables in her hands, a row of angry, shocked faces looming above her. 'I just wanted to see what kind of hardware was inside, that's all. My Uncle Henry says that taking something apart is the best way—'

'Well, that is a very silly thing for your uncle to say,' interrupted Mrs Wright sharply. 'At our school we do *not* take things apart, we leave them *exactly* as we found them. Goodness me, young lady, your uncle has taught you some strange things.'

Alex spent the rest of the morning willing the final bell to ring. School wasn't at all what she'd expected. She'd imagined a place of wonderful scholarship, with twinkly-eyed teachers who knew *everything* there was to know about *everything*. In her head, she'd seen them scrawling madly at blackboards in fits of mathematical passion, conducting dangerous experiments to uncover the deepest secrets of the universe, giving enlightening sermons about history, philosophy and science with easy charm and wit – all in the noble pursuit of expanding young minds. The reality, however, was quite different.

To be fair to the teachers of Murford College – who were in fact very competent educators by normal standards – this fantasy was a little unreasonable. But Alex was disappointed, nonetheless.

And yet, if she was honest, this wasn't the real reason for her sadness. Because more than anything else she'd imagined at school, Alex had imagined friends. Maybe even a *best friend*. Somebody to chat to and ask questions. To laugh with at things that nobody else in the world thought were funny. She'd heard about friends like that. But she'd never had one of her own.

Having spent most of her childhood with only her uncle for company, Alex wasn't exactly sure how one went about making friends. She remembered a television documentary she'd once watched that recommended using something called *conversation starters*. Following this advice, after lunch she leaned over to the girl at the next desk with her best smile.

'Hello,' she whispered. 'What's your favourite number and why?' To her dismay, the girl looked puzzled, shrugged and shifted her desk several inches away.

A little wounded, but undeterred, Alex tried again at the end of class. She caught up to a broad-shouldered boy who had sat in front of her in maths.

'I couldn't help but notice,' she began, excitedly, 'that you can wiggle your ears. Did you know you were doing it? That's quite rare in humans. You probably inherited it from your parents. Not many humans can do it. Rats can, I think, and cows are really good at it . . .'

Alex stopped talking. She noticed the expression on the boy's face. It looked like he had gargled vinegar. 'Are you . . . saying I look like a cow?' he spluttered.

'No!' Alex choked. 'Of course not. I was only saying . . . I think it's really cool that you can wiggle your ears like a cow.'

She thought for a horrible second that the boy might hit her. Or, even worse, start to cry. But instead he pressed his hands firmly to his ears and hurried in the direction of the boys' toilets.

Alex wasn't quite sure where she'd gone wrong, but she decided not to try any more friend-making attempts for the rest of the day.

When the last bell finally rang, Alex felt exhausted. The last thing she wanted to see as she traipsed across the playground towards the school gates was the white double-decker coach.

Its passengers were standing like a picket line between the gates, chatting animatedly amongst themselves. A teacher in a high visibility vest was shouting and waving frantically at the driver who ignored the performance completely. When Alex reached the gates, however, the crowd of tourists hushed and quickly parted for her. She walked hastily through the centre, ignoring the whispers that followed her. And then she ran the whole way home.

*

News spread quickly about the unfortunate incidents on Alex's first day at school. Not long after, her classmates started calling her names like *weirdo* and *geek* and avoided her at break times. The teachers weren't very impressed with her either because of her tendency to lose her homework. Though she worked hard on it every night, somehow on the walk to school it disappeared from her bag. Of course, none of the teachers believed her that her workbooks vanished into thin air. Who would want to pinch a child's homework?

Alex's experiences at school made her feel, like her uncle, very confused by the behaviour of other people. For instance, when it was announced one day that her class was to put on a play, as a fundraiser for the local animal sanctuary, she thought it extremely odd that nearly all her classmates wanted the starring role. The prospect of standing up on stage in front of hundreds of people made her legs turn to jelly. Though she explained this to her teachers – and even offered to do double maths homework for a month instead – they wouldn't listen.

'I can't do it, Uncle Henry,' she cried that evening. 'I'll fall on my face. I'll forget my lines. I'll be the worst llama that any school play has ever had! Everyone will laugh at me.'

'Well, in that case,' Henry said, chuckling fondly, 'I'd better get my ticket. The worst llama in all of history sounds like something I don't want to miss.' At this, Alex couldn't help but smile. Her uncle always had a way of making her feel better.

*

Backstage on opening night, dressed head to toe in itchy, beige-coloured fur, Alex thought quite seriously about escaping out of a first-floor window. She peeked through thick red curtains to see Uncle Henry sitting in the third row, fiddling with a video camera he had modified to have an extra-long zoom.

As she looked at the rows behind him, Alex had to steady herself. The hall was full to bursting. Every seat was taken, sometimes twice. One rather muscular gentleman was perched on the lap of a much smaller man, who struggled to see beyond his companion's rippling arms. People knelt in the aisle and huddled at the back of the hall, spilling out along the corridor. Some even stood at the windows, pressed to the glass with binoculars tight to their faces as if they were at the opera.

Alex couldn't believe that a school play would be so

popular and, judging by their expressions of mild alarm, neither could her teachers.

When Alex shuffled on stage near the end of the first act, a bristle of excitement crossed the hall. After her first and only line, an audible gasp came from somewhere in the back row, which made her hurriedly check that her tights hadn't slipped down and her pointy llama ears were still firmly in place.

Then, during a particularly energetic group dance number, Alex tripped over her own feet and almost fell clean off the stage. A shocked silence gripped the hall. When she stood up again, there was a roar of thunderous clapping. Emotional cries of 'Brava! Brava!' broke out from those squatting in the aisle. Somebody – she didn't see who – tossed a bouquet of red roses at her feet.

The other children on stage looked suspiciously at Alex. The parents in the audience clapped louder for their own children, hooting and hollering over each other until the play was more raucous than a football match. Only Uncle Henry noticed nothing out of the ordinary, watching through the long lens of his camera, which for most of the play was zoomed into Alex's left foot.

*

Time passed, but Alex still didn't make any friends. Incidents like the school play didn't help. Though Uncle Henry wasn't surprised to hear about the peculiar behaviour of her peers, he was terribly sad to see his niece so disappointed. He wanted very much to help Alex solve the problem of *making friends* but simply had no idea how. Until, in her fourth week at school, Uncle Henry announced that he had finally found a solution.

'Your twelfth birthday is this weekend,' he said. 'And it says here that some people like to celebrate birthdays by throwing a party.' He was scrolling through an article describing how to make friends, looking somewhat unconvinced. 'It says here that most people like parties. That they even *enjoy* them. Well, good heavens. I suppose if that's the case, that's what we'll do. We'll have to move some things,' he added, looking around their small living room, 'But I'm sure we can fit everyone here. Gosh, how exciting, I've never hosted a party before. I've never *been* to a party before.'

Though the idea of a birthday party made her nervous, Alex passed around invitations the next day at school. She was relieved when people took them, though she did get a few surprised looks. One boy even asked if she was new, saying he hadn't seen her around before, and Alex was too embarrassed to explain that she'd been sitting behind him in class for almost a month.

On the day of the party, Uncle Henry and Alex woke early. They vacuumed the carpets, they dusted the living room furniture and Henry even reluctantly stuffed his video games under his bed. Afterwards, they moved on to the kitchen, a room in the house they seldom visited under normal circumstances, except to cook baked beans on toast, which more often than not they burned.

'I like baking,' Uncle Henry announced an hour later, flour in his hair, down his T-shirt and somehow on the tip of his nose. 'With all those ingredients it's a bit like a chemistry experiment.'

Alex agreed with her uncle, though she rather hoped the cake wouldn't *taste* like a chemistry experiment.

Miraculously, the cake emerged from the oven golden brown and perfectly round. They placed it next to a spread of fizzy sweets and beige-coloured food, which the website had recommended they buy, and bowls of their own favourite snack, pickled eggs. Alex cut out paper bunting from old computer manuals Uncle Henry kept around the house and hung it up in every room. Together, they devised some party games involving times tables.

'This website suggests something called musical bumps,' Uncle Henry frowned. 'But all that running around sounds quite dangerous if you ask me.'

By the time everything was ready, it was nearly half-past three – thirty minutes before the party was due to start. As they waited for the guests to arrive, Alex became very hot. Her stomach did somersaults in her belly as if she'd swallowed a small dolphin. She found it impossible to sit still and so moved from room to room, straightening picture frames that were already perfectly straight. Every thirty seconds she glanced at the clock on the wall. The minute hand crept past half three. And then quarter to. Finally, it was four o'clock. Her head flashed towards the door hopefully but there were no knocks. The dolphin jumping in her belly turned suddenly to cement. She straightened more pictures. It was quarter past four. Then half past. The sight of her uncle returning yet again to the sausage roll platter made her quite cross.

'Don't eat everything just yet!' Henry had wolfed down the last of the sausage rolls and a handful of scotch eggs. 'They could still come.'

But soon, the light began to fade in the living room, and along with it all hope that anyone was coming.

'We must have put the wrong date on the invitation.'

Uncle Henry was pacing the room with his hands behind his back.

Alex didn't believe him – she knew her uncle would never get a number wrong – but his face was so sad she pretended to.

'Silly us.' She gave him her best smile. 'More cake for me and you.'

Alex had a hollow feeling in her chest as she started clearing away the bowls of food and popping balloons one by one. With every bang of bursting rubber, she felt even more miserable. She would never get her hopes up about something as foolish as a party ever again. She was halfway up a ladder untying bunting from the curtain rail when she heard a noise that sounded like one of her uncle's computer games.

Brrrriiinng brrrriiinng.

For a moment, Alex didn't move.

Brrrriiinng brrrriiinng.

The second time she heard it there was no doubt about what it was.

'We have a doorbell?' she said to herself, climbing down the ladder two steps at a time.

At the door, Alex hesitated. Her hair, which she had brushed out for the party, now sat in its usual messy half-sprout on top of her head. Taking down the decorations had given her a sweaty glow. She wondered who might be at the door – deep down she hoped that it was the popular girls in her class, though she hadn't actually been brave enough to give them invitations. Through the clouded glass of the door she could make out a single, blurry shape. Hesitantly, she twisted the lock and slid her head through the opening.

There, illuminated in the pale-yellow porchlight, stood a boy. He was around her age, with thick black hair standing up straight towards the sky.

'Alex,' he said, breathlessly, holding out a hand for her to shake. 'My name is Jasper. I hope I'm not too late.'

CHAPTER THREE

Gatecrasher

For a few seconds, the pair stood in total silence. The boy was very tall and thin. He wore a pea-green suit with a shiny waistcoat and thick black boots, which, though she cared little about fashion, Alex thought was an odd combination. He was panting as if he'd been running and his skin shone with sweat.

She recounted the names of her classmates in her head, then the names of those in the year above, and the year above that. Alex remembered all the elements in the periodic table. She knew the names of all the rivers in South America. She'd never once forgotten a face. So, she had no doubt that this boy was a complete stranger.

'Jasper who?' Alex said, a little more forcefully than she intended.

'Jasper Song,' he said, beaming.

'Well, Jasper Song, you must have the wrong house.'
She retreated behind the door like a snail into its shell.
'Sorry . . . thanks . . . bye.'

'No, I'm sure this is the right house,' replied the boy,
stopping the door gently with his hand. 'I just moved
in a few streets away. And I heard you were having a
party. I don't know anyone yet, so I thought I'd stop by
and say hello. Your name is Alex, isn't it? It is your
birthday today?'

Alex stared dumbly back. Though he couldn't be
more than twelve, the boy spoke with the authority
of a police officer. His face was locked in a serious
expression, but she sensed he might break into a smile
at any moment.

'Oh – um – yes. It is my birthday.' Alex blinked to
steady her vision. She was still using the half-open door
as a shield between them. 'But how did you know that?'

'I have this.' He waved a slip of paper on which she
recognised the slant of her uncle's handwriting. It was
one of her party invitations.

'But . . . where did you get *that*?'

'Oh – er – I found it.' For a moment he didn't sound
quite as confident as he had before, like he was in a
play and had forgotten his lines.

Alex frowned in disbelief. She supposed she could

have dropped an invitation on her way home from school or, more likely, one of her classmates had dropped theirs. But how had this boy come to find it? And why would he decide to turn up when he didn't even know her? She noticed him glance towards the street and then quickly back. It seemed as if he was expecting someone else, but as far as she could see they were completely alone.

'So,' Jasper smiled. 'Have I passed the test? Can I come in?'

Minutes later, the boy was sitting bolt upright on the sofa. Alex and Uncle Henry were keeping a safe distance away, whispering to each other in the corner like a couple of zookeepers discussing how to approach a hungry tiger.

'He likes pickled eggs,' Uncle Henry murmured, as they watched Jasper reach for his second helping. 'That's a good sign in my books. And he called me "sir"! Can you imagine that?'

Alex crossed her arms. 'But it doesn't make sense, Uncle Henry. We've never even met. Do people normally go to complete stranger's birthday parties?'

'Never mind that. He's our *guest*.' Henry's voice was higher than normal and he was talking fast, like he did when a new comic book arrived in the post. 'And though I'm no expert in social etiquette, I think we're being a little bit rude. Go on, offer the boy some cake. He clearly has a good appetite.'

Uncle Henry gave her a prod in between her shoulder blades and sunk into his favourite armchair. He buried his nose in a copy of *An Introduction to Particle Physics* and pretended to start reading.

Her uncle's eyes followed her from above the pages of his book as Alex cut two slices of cake and placed them carefully on a napkin. Across the room, Jasper had taken a book out of his bag and begun to read. Despite his stiff posture, he didn't seem bored or annoyed by their rudeness; on the contrary, he had the expression of someone lost within another world entirely.

Edging towards him, Alex cleared her throat. 'Cake?' She spoke much louder than she'd intended. 'We dropped the saltshaker in the batter by mistake, so it's a little salty, but it's not actually too bad if you—'

Before she could finish her sentence, Jasper threw his book aside and took the largest slice out of her hands. He ate the sponge in a few bites, then took the other slice too. When he finished, he looked back at her with sticky red jam smeared across his mouth and cheeks.

Alex fought the urge to laugh. He certainly *seemed* harmless, she thought, watching Jasper lick cake crumbs from his fingers one by one. But she had to be careful. Though he was just a boy, he was a stranger. And in her mind, nothing was more unpredictable. Given the choice, in fact, she would have preferred a hungry tiger to a hungry human boy. At least there were books she could have read about how to approach a tiger – what a flick of her tail meant, or the position of her head, or the signals which meant you should run for your life. There was no guidebook for Jasper Song; Alex had to work him out all by herself.

And the more Alex thought about it, the less his story made sense. Who turns up out of the blue at a complete stranger's birthday party? There had to be more to it than Jasper was letting on. But what? And *why*? She watched carefully as Jasper wiped jam from his mouth with his napkin. He leaned back into the sofa and sighed. 'That was the best cake I've ever had,' he announced. 'The salt made my tongue tingle. You're a very good baker.'

Alex felt pleased, despite her best effort not to. 'It was mostly my uncle,' she replied, embarrassed. 'But I'm glad you liked it.' In the silence that followed, Alex searched for something to say. Her attempts at small talk never seemed to go very well. 'You like to read?' she said finally, nodding at the hardback lying upturned on the sofa.

Jasper retrieved his abandoned book. 'It's a classic,' he told her, proudly. 'I love old books, the older the better. Especially those with really faded covers and yellow pages. They smell amazing. I always keep one with me.'

'Oh, me too,' mumbled Alex. That wasn't strictly true. She mostly preferred reading new books about new things: she loved books about the latest gadgets and mind-blowing, futuristic inventions. Or books that taught her things about the world: books about spiders, or snakes, or the Egyptian pharaoh Tutankhamun. Still, Alex was reassured to hear that Jasper liked books as much as she did. 'What's it called?' she asked.

'*The Secret Garden.*'

'Is it about gardening?'

Jasper laughed. It was a kind laugh, the sort that spreads cheeriness around a room. 'Not really,' he said. 'There is a garden, a lovely garden. But I think it's mostly about . . . friendship.'

'Friendship,' repeated Alex, as if it was the most serious subject in the world. 'I don't think I've ever read a book about friendship before. Is it good?'

'Yes, very good.' A thoughtful expression came over Jasper's face. He looked down at the book, flicking through its pages, before nodding. 'You can have it if you like.'

Alex took a step back. 'Have it?' she said. 'Oh, I couldn't. Don't you want to finish it?'

'I've read it millions of times before.' Jasper waved his hand as if to say *it's nothing*. 'Call it a birthday present. Sorry it's not wrapped.' He held the book out to her. 'Go on, please.'

His manner was so decisive Alex felt she couldn't possibly refuse. Her face went hot. She'd never been given a birthday present before by anyone except for her uncle, and his presents were usually video games or socks.

'Thank you.' She traced her finger over the cloth-bound cover. It was a beautiful object, with curly writing that swept across the front and a border of shiny gold flowers. Alex took a deep breath. It was difficult to take everything in. Not half an hour ago, she had been bursting balloons and taking down bunting. Now she stood holding a birthday present from a boy she'd only just met. She wanted to be grateful, but her head was still swimming with questions. 'So, Jasper,' she began hesitantly. 'Where did you move here from?'

'A very, very long way away.' His hands sunk into the sides of his waistcoat. 'Scotland, in fact!' There was an expression on his face of someone who had remembered a private joke.

'Scotland,' she repeated. 'I've never been there but I'd really like to go. Why did you move to Murford?'

'For a job,' he said. 'I mean . . . my parents. They have jobs here. Not me obviously.'

'I guess that makes sense,' Alex admitted. Jasper smiled widely, unbuttoning his waistcoat and sinking back into the sofa cushions. Another person might have taken this moment to ask Jasper about his strange outfit, but Alex was far too polite. Besides that, she'd never cared much about the clothes people wore. Truth be told, now she was getting used to it, she very much liked the pea-greenness of his suit and admired the gold thread on his waistcoat. She swept her finger across the stitching on her new book, building the nerve to ask the question that was really bothering her.

When she finally did, it came out as a quick jumble of words. 'What made you decide to come to *my* party?'

'I don't know.' Jasper shrugged, and he looked genuinely unsure. 'I just did. You know how an idea jumps into your head? Don't you ever act impulsively? Act first and think later?'

Now it was Alex's turn to laugh. Jasper clearly didn't know who he was talking to. Alex barely crossed the road without first conducting a thorough health and safety assessment. She prided herself on being rational, on thinking through every *if* and *but* and *maybe* imaginable before making a decision. Ideas didn't so much jump into her head as audition to be there.

Alex started to explain this to Jasper when the sound of soft, rhythmic snores drifted from the armchair across the room. Her uncle's mouth lolled open and the book rested on the tip of his nose.

'Let's go outside,' Alex whispered to Jasper, 'and leave him to sleep.'

She placed her book carefully on the table, picked up a bowl of sweets and tiptoed through the double doors that led to the small garden behind the house, with Jasper following. They sat on the patio steps, passing back and forth the bowl of fizzy sweets and listening to the traffic rushing beyond the garden fence. The stars were starting to come out and a breeze rustled the small overgrown patch of grass which stretched to the end of the garden.

Alex leaned backwards on to the patio, cold stone under her palms. Jasper did the same, though the position looked quite uncomfortable in his suit. His trouser legs rose at the ankles revealing bright striped socks beneath his boots. She noticed that they weren't a matching pair and smiled approvingly.

'You like my socks?' Jasper's eyes lit up. 'I think pairing socks is a complete waste of time, don't you? They do the same job whatever pattern or colour they are. Why do people go to all that trouble?'

'I completely agree,' replied Alex. 'My uncle does too. We like logical arguments. Especially if they get us out of boring things, like pairing socks.'

They fell into a thoughtful silence, chewing their way through the bowl of sweets. Her eyes wandered up to the night sky, as they often did. It was the colour of spilled blue ink. Looking at it, Alex felt suddenly restless.

Jasper threw another gummy worm up into the air and caught it with his mouth. 'Penny for your thoughts.'

'Oh, nothing.'

'Go on. I'm tall ears.'

'You're . . . *tall ears*?'

'Is that not the saying?' He looked embarrassed. 'Thought it sounded a bit strange. But then most sayings do.'

'Oh, you mean you're *all ears*.' Alex grinned. Jasper really was a bit odd, she thought. But she decided she didn't mind. After all, everyone at school thought *she* was odd. And it was a weird saying. 'Well – don't laugh – but I was thinking about something my uncle once told me.'

'Go on.'

'Apparently,' she began, 'there are more stars in the sky than there are grains of sand on all the beaches in the world.'

'All the beaches?'

'Yep, every single one. There are *billions* of stars and planets. The Earth is one tiny dot amongst them. And there's still so much about the universe that we don't know. Like what happens in a black hole, and how time works, and whether there's life out there apart from us. Maybe there are creatures who right this second are looking back at us and wondering the same. Uncle Henry and I look for them sometimes with our telescope.'

'Hmmm,' was all Jasper said.

Alex worried she'd said something weird again, like she often did at school. She was just starting to like him and now he'd soon be making excuses to leave and she'd have ruined her first chance to make a real friend. She watched him nervously from the corner of her vision as he scratched his chin.

'These aliens . . . do you think they are partial to gummy worms too?'

Alex laughed with relief. 'Yes, definitely.'

'But I bet alien gummy worms are ginormous.'

'Yeah,' she said, laughing, 'the size of your arm.'

'The size of your leg!'

'And they wriggle around all over the place and you have to catch them to eat them.'

'Now that's gross,' he said, and they both laughed. A police siren was getting louder and louder as it approached the street behind the house. Alex's thoughts were suddenly brought back down to earth.

She sighed. 'I bet at alien birthday parties people actually turn up,' she said once the siren had passed. 'Even with giant worms wriggling everywhere.'

'If you ask me, parties are way overrated,' said Jasper. 'All those people and all that noise – it gives me a headache. I'd prefer to have a conversation about alien gummy worms any day.'

Alex stared back at Jasper for a moment longer than was polite. She searched his face for a hint that he might be making fun of her. There had been moments at school when Alex had believed someone was being nice, only to realise that they were making fun of her all along. Jasper was oblivious, his head craned up at the sky.

'Do you know what I like most about the stars?'

Jasper sighed. 'That they never really change. Even the dinosaurs were looking up at a sky that looked just like this. I've always found that kind of comforting.'

Before Alex could open her mouth to reply, there was a rustling sound at the end of the garden. At first, it sounded like her neighbour's cat, Orlando, a fat tabby who often got stuck in the hole beneath the fence. Then there was the sound of broken twigs and a dull thud which suggested something much bigger than a cat.

She turned towards Jasper. His body was rigid. The carefree look on his face had been replaced with something much darker. There was another crashing sound and a muffled yelp.

'Ouch!' came a hushed voice from the other side of the fence. 'That was my foot!'

'Well, your head,' came another whispered voice, 'is completely blocking my view.'

'What exactly would you like me to do with my head, dear? Shall I set it down on the ground? Would that be better for you?'

Alex frowned in the way she did when an equation wasn't working out right. Behind her garden fence was only a small, dark passageway barely wide enough for a thin person to walk through sideways. Her neighbours, meanwhile, were very elderly and unlikely to be scaling her fence late at night.

'Doesn't she look grown up?' continued the first voice. 'She's twice the size she was last November.'

'Quiet, Vera. She'll hear us, then we really will be in trouble. Remember last time, when—'

The double doors to the living room swung open with a bang. There stood her uncle holding a piece of cake pierced with twelve glowing candles. The rustling at the end of the garden fell immediately silent.

Uncle Henry cleared his throat loudly. 'Happy birthday to you, happy birthday . . .'

His voice wobbled high and low between the notes. On the third line, Jasper joined in and the two half-sung, half-shouted their way to the end of the song. Even though they were both terribly out of tune – and the candles were dangerously close to collapsing – Alex beamed with pride. As she blew out the flames, her uncle and Jasper cheered wildly, and she forgot all about the voices at the end of the garden.

CHAPTER FOUR

New Boy in Class

Jasper started at Alex's school the very next day. When Mrs Wright brought him into registration, Alex couldn't help but notice the strange effect he had on her classmates. New children always got a lot of attention when they joined the class, and the green suit he wore certainly made him stand out. But there was something different about the way the class reacted to Jasper compared to how they'd treated Alex when *she'd* first started.

She quickly realized what the difference was: they thought he was *cool*. It was something to do with the way he stood out but didn't seem to care, and with the confident way he held himself and smiled. Even Mrs Wright was acting peculiarly, her voice softer and face less hawkish than usual.

'Here we are, dear,' she said, folding her arms beneath her bosom. 'Take a seat at the back, there's a good lad.'

Jasper walked to a free desk a few rows behind Alex, giving her a small salute as he passed.

'This is Jasper Song. Jasper has joined us from Scotland, isn't that right?' continued Mrs Wright, her manicured hands clasped together. 'Now, I'm sure you're all very excited to have a new student in the class, and that everyone will make him welcome. And I must say it *is* refreshing to see a young man dressed so smartly for school. Your suit doesn't quite fit in with our uniform policy, but we won't worry about that on your first day.'

A few minutes later, when Jasper put up his hand to say that he needed a pen, all the girls in the class rummaged around in their pencil cases as if digging for gold. He took one from a girl sitting at the desk next to him and her eyes glazed over like she was about to faint. The boys too, Alex noticed, were sitting straighter in their seats, sizing him up when they thought no one was looking.

The bell for break rang and most of the class rushed towards the door. Those that remained gathered in a small crowd around Jasper, who was packing his books into his satchel.

'I'll show you round, if you like.' A small girl at the front of the crowd was twisting her fingers through the ends of her dark, curly hair. 'My grandma was Scottish. You can tell me what it's like to live there.'

The girl's name was Isabella. Her face was as beautiful as her name suggested and she had a clear, high-pitched voice, which she often used to talk over others in class. In that moment, as she waited for Jasper's answer, Isabella looked the picture of sweetness.

Jasper smiled and swung his satchel across his body. Alex's heart sank. She knew that once Jasper became friends with Isabella, he would never want to spend time with her. She didn't want to hang around to watch it happen. Alex sloped towards the door.

She was halfway down the corridor when Jasper caught up.

'Hey!' he called. 'Where are you going?'

Alex hesitated. 'To the computer room.'

'Can I come too?'

Her mouth fell open. 'But aren't you getting a tour from Isabella?'

'Oh, no,' he said. 'I told her I had plans.'

'You told her you had plans?' Alex repeated, disbelieving. 'She's pretty popular here, you know. I'm not sure it's wise to turn her down.'

He wrinkled his nose. 'What makes you think I want to be popular?'

'Don't most people?'

'Not me,' he said. 'At my school – my old school I mean – most people thought I was a bit strange and that was fine by me. Being popular always looks kind of exhausting.'

It turned out Jasper wasn't very good at using the computer. In fact, Alex thought, he treated it like he'd never even seen one before. He put his ear to the back of the screen as if listening for something inside. He shook the mouse so hard the little ball rolled out on to the floor. And he laughed for ten minutes straight after Alex showed him how to type on the keyboard. Under his breath she heard him mutter things like *just amazing* and *absolutely unbelievable*. She told him that she could show him what was inside the computer, but it would make the teachers very angry. In the end he was happy to read some chapters of a book while she practised a new kind of coding.

As the day went on, Jasper stayed by Alex's side. When Jasper was invited to play a game of football in the playground at lunch, he said he would rather accompany Alex to the library. In the afternoon, Jasper turned down Isabella's invitation to be her science partner. He said he was already partnered with Alex. When the final bell rang, they left the school gates together. In fact, Jasper insisted on walking with Alex all the way to her house.

On the walk home, Jasper asked her a thousand questions. Like, what was her favourite way to eat eggs. And would she prefer to have three arms or twenty fingers. He listened carefully, as if making a mental note of her answers. Alex found this very odd; whenever she spoke to people in her class they would stare at her blankly, then turn to each other and share a look which Alex knew meant *she's weird*. She wanted to ask Jasper some questions in return, like where he lived, and what Scotland was like, but found she never had the chance.

When they arrived at Alex's house, her uncle insisted Jasper stay for dinner. 'So long as it's OK with your parents,' he said, as an afterthought. 'Perhaps we should give them a call?'

'Don't worry about that. Because . . . because . . . they're away on business,' Jasper said.

Most adults would be shocked at the idea of a twelve year old being left home alone. But Uncle Henry wasn't a normal kind of adult. 'How nice,' he said, stirring the pan of beans. 'What do they do?'

'They are . . .' Jasper paused, looking up at the ceiling. Alex leaned in closer to hear his answer. He was like a puzzle with half the pieces missing and she was eager to complete the picture. 'Dentists. Both of them,' he said finally.

'What an interesting profession.' Uncle Henry handed them each a plate of beans on toast and they headed into the living room. 'Do they enjoy looking in other people's mouths?'

'I guess they must do,' Jasper said, sitting down.

'Are they very strict about sugar?' asked Alex.

'Huh?'

'Your parents. Being dentists, I mean.'

Jasper's eyes widened. 'Oh, yeah, yeah. Strict. Very.' He spooned so many baked beans into his mouth his cheeks bulged. 'But your job is much more interesting than theirs, Henry,' he said, still chewing. 'Tell me again about that spreadsheet you mentioned earlier. It sounded fascinating.'

This was all the encouragement Uncle Henry needed to talk for the rest of the meal about his work. Jasper sat back with a look of relief. Alex stared at him curiously across the living room as they ate the meal on their laps. For a boy who loved asking other people questions, he was an expert at avoiding them himself.

She wanted to interrupt to ask where exactly his parents were and when they were coming back. But once her uncle started telling a story there was little she could do to stop him.

After dinner, they introduced Jasper to the games console. Jasper was terrible at all the games but listened enthusiastically to Uncle Henry talking about the quality of the graphics. In turn, he told them all about his favourite books, reeling off a long list of titles.

'At my last school they didn't really like us to read books for fun,' he explained. 'They only wanted you to read books to learn things about the time they were written in. Like what people wore or how they spoke. They wanted us to spot differences between the book's time and our own. But I just like to get lost in the story.'

'Is that a common approach in Scotland, Jasper?' asked Uncle Henry.

Jasper hesitated. 'No. My school was very different to most schools. It's an unusual place. Too strict if you ask me.'

'Where exactly in Scotland was your school?' asked Alex, eagerly.

'Oh, in the north,' Jasper said. 'Far north. Middle of nowhere really. You wouldn't find it easily on a map.'

He stared intently out the window, as if the lamp post across the road was suddenly captivating.

Alex frowned. There were loose threads in Jasper's story. Things that didn't make sense. But if she started pulling at those loose threads, Alex worried that everything might start to unravel. Their friendship – so new and fragile – might fall apart as quickly as it had formed. So, Alex pushed her questions away. She tried to ignore her doubts and allow herself to enjoy it – her first real friendship.

*

Over the next few weeks, walking home from school together became routine for Jasper and Alex. On the journey, they talked and talked, and then talked some more. When Alex finished reading *The Secret Garden*, they discussed their favourite parts. Alex loved the descriptions of the garden best. Jasper, on the other hand, said he liked the way the characters changed for the better. Jasper told Alex about other books he'd read, stories about pirates and chocolate factories and jungle adventures. And he listened attentively as Alex talked about things like how steam trains work and why kangaroos can't walk backwards.

'Did you know,' asked Alex one day, as they left the school gates, 'that jellyfish don't have brains?'

Jasper looked amazed. 'But how do they think?' he replied. 'Or move their tentacles? Does that mean they're basically zombies?' Before Alex could explain, Jasper began his best impression of a zombie jellyfish. He stuck his arms out and wobbled his whole body. 'Join me!' he commanded in an extra-wobbly zombie voice. Alex hesitated. Her eyes darted to the group of popular girls across the road. 'Come on, Alex!' he insisted. 'Let your inner zombie jellyfish take over.'

Reluctantly, Alex raised her tentacles. If Jasper didn't care what the popular girls thought, then why should she? The pair wobbled side by side the whole way home. They were laughing so much when they arrived that they couldn't speak, not even to explain the joke to poor, perplexed Uncle Henry.

At school, Alex and Jasper quickly became inseparable. They sat next to one another in most lessons. If the class was asked to pair up, Alex knew without thinking who her partner would be. Even the most boring lessons became fun with Jasper around. He sketched dangerously accurate cartoons of teachers in his workbooks, making them both shake with suppressed laughter. Unlike Alex, he was never worried about getting into trouble; to Jasper, rules were more like guidelines, or challenges.

It took a month for other students to stop following him in the corridor. But eventually, everybody ignored Jasper as they did Alex. And that suited them perfectly.

Having somebody to talk to for the first time made Alex feel wonderful. She shared her thoughts and feelings, fears and worries, knowing Jasper would understand. She felt she could talk to him about anything in the world. Almost. There was just one exception.

Whenever she asked Jasper a personal question – like where he was born, or whether he had any siblings – he mumbled something vague and quickly changed the subject. It bothered Alex that, despite all their conversations, she didn't know a single thing about his life before he moved to Murford. She'd never been to his house or met his parents. His past was a complete mystery. It couldn't be that he was shy; he was the most confident person she'd ever met. *Was he embarrassed about his family?* Or perhaps it was the other way around? Maybe he was embarrassed of *her* . . .

One evening after dinner, Alex decided to corner him. Jasper was standing in the hallway getting ready to leave. He had one boot on and was tugging at the other. Her uncle was safely out of earshot.

'Jasper,' said Alex, trying to sound casual. 'Tomorrow, what if we go to your house after school instead? Just for a change. You must be sick of baked beans by now.'

Jasper's face went stiff. It was the same look he got whenever Alex asked questions about his past. 'No, really sorry but we can't.' He tugged more urgently at his boot.

Alex tried not to show it, but she was hurt. She couldn't help but feel she'd done something wrong. 'But why not?' she asked.

'We just can't. My place is boring anyway. And I'd *never* get tired of baked beans.'

'Yes, but . . .' She tried to choose her words carefully. She wished Jasper was a machine she could open up and see what was inside, but human boys didn't work like that. She had to find another way. 'You never talk about your family. I don't know if you have brothers or sisters, or even where you live. You *say* your parents are dentists, but I've never known dentists who travel quite as much as yours do.'

'Alex, please.' He checked behind him before carrying on in a whisper. 'My parents *are* dentists.

They just . . . go away a lot for work. There's no mystery to solve.'

'But—'

'Listen,' he interrupted. 'I can't talk about it any more. Or . . . or . . . they'll send me back to Scotland. They'll make me leave Murford for good.'

'Who will?' gasped Alex.

Jasper didn't answer straight away. 'My parents,' he said eventually. 'Who else?'

Alex couldn't bear the thought that Jasper might leave. And yet . . . she really didn't like being lied to. 'I don't think,' Alex began, nervously, 'that you're telling me the whole truth. I think there's something you're not saying.'

Jasper turned away. 'Just forget about it.'

Alex took a deep breath. It wasn't in her nature to let things go.

'Friends share things,' she said. 'They tell each other the truth.'

'It's not that simple.'

'It's perfectly simple,' she said, hotly. She wasn't quite shouting, but very nearly.

Jasper's eyes were on the floor. 'I can't.'

'Maybe,' Alex said angrily, 'maybe, we aren't really friends then.'

Alex was as shocked as Jasper by what she'd said. There was a ten-second silence, ample opportunity for her to take back her words, which she certainly didn't mean. But she let it pass, staring resolutely at the wall. Jasper gave an anguished sigh, opened the front door and walked slowly out into the night.

Alex watched him walk, head down, all the way to the end of the street. He didn't look back.

CHAPTER FIVE

The Vanishing Woman

The next morning, Jasper wasn't at registration. He missed double maths and music too. By breaktime, Alex was sick with worry. Where was he? She thought over and over about what she'd said the night before. Why had she tried to force answers out of him? Why couldn't she have just let it go? Now, she'd lost her first ever friend. And she only had herself to blame.

The final class before lunch was a careers lesson. Alex's heart sank as Mrs Wright marked Jasper down as absent and closed the door to begin.

'Quiet!' she shouted from her desk at the front. 'Quiet! I have a treat for you all today. We are going to do a little test.' There was a collective groan from everyone except for Alex, who was far too miserable to care about a test. 'None of that silliness!' barked the teacher. 'Now, take one and pass it on, quickly, quickly. This isn't any old examination. This is a careers test! It will tell you what career you are destined to have when you're grown up.' The class shared looks of genuine interest as the papers spread around the room. 'You have twenty minutes to give your answers. And you will do so in complete silence. Pass them to the front when you're done. Now, go!'

The class eagerly picked up their pens and got to work. Alex sat and stared at the piece of paper, her pencil hovering like a wandering cloud over its pages, while her classmates drew large and enthusiastic crosses until their papers looked like constellations of stars across a night sky. They didn't realise what Alex understood: that their teachers were astrologers, reading the stars for their destiny. Each cross shifted them like a speeding train on to another track, another future. Alex wasn't very interested in her future now that Jasper was gone. Besides, she didn't want to be a train stuck on a track. So, she didn't cross any boxes at all.

There was a low murmur of discussion as the class waited for their results. Alex rested her head on her elbow, staring at the drizzly sky through the window. *Could Jasper have gone back to Scotland already?* she wondered. Surely, it took longer than a night to move countries, to change schools. If he'd been at school, he would have cheered her up about the test. They would have made fun of it together afterwards. Alex kept one eye on the door. It didn't move. *Where is he?* she thought again with a louder-than-intended sigh.

'You are right to sigh, my girl,' came a booming voice from the front of the room. 'You failed to answer a single question! Completely blank! What on earth were you doing all that time?'

Mrs Wright held Alex's test paper high above her head. Alex slid lower down in her seat, wishing she was invisible.

'Don't you want to be anything?' Mrs Wright's jowls shook with indignation. 'Do you want to be a nobody? Alex Nobody, shall we call you?' Laughter echoed around the classroom.

Mrs Wright continued tutting at Alex as she padded from desk to desk handing back the rest of the papers. It turned out the class was full of important people: lawyers, politicians, journalists. Isabella announced that she was to be a television presenter, and the class dutifully responded with impressed looks and sounds.

'Nice one, Alex Nobody,' Isabella said to Alex in a loud whisper. 'If you like, you can have my autograph.

It will probably be worth a fortune when I'm famous and on television.' The class laughed and Isabella looked very pleased with herself. Mrs Wright was close enough to have heard but said nothing. Isabella handed Alex a page of her notebook signed with the words *For Alex Nobody* above her swirly signature.

Alex stared resolutely at her desk. They were right. She was Alex Nobody. Everybody at school thought so, even her teachers. Everybody except for Jasper, and now he was gone. And it was her fault. Red hot tears built in her eyes. She wanted to run home and never leave the house again. Everything Uncle Henry had said about the world was true.

That moment, something hit Alex's shoulder. Now Isabella was throwing things, she thought, and she hunched low over her desk. Alex waited to hear the usual sniggers, except this time there were none. Instead, there was a low hissing sound coming from the back of the classroom.

Composing her face, she swivelled round. At the far open window was a head of sticking-up black hair and two dark eyes. Alex almost jumped right out her seat. *Jasper!* Her body flooded with relief. He hadn't left for ever. He wasn't back in Scotland. He was *here*! But then . . . why wasn't he in class? And what was he doing at the window? Jasper gave a small wave and pointed towards a piece of scrunched paper on the floor.

It was a note.

In all the excitement about the careers test results it was easy for Alex to reach for the note unnoticed. Smoothing the paper out across her desk, she read the words written in slanted green ink:

Meet me outside the front gate at 1. I'll tell you everything. Jasper.

There were two reasons why this was a strange meeting place for Jasper to suggest. Firstly, it was raining, the fine kind of rain which you hardly notice but soaks you in minutes. Second, students were strictly forbidden from leaving school grounds at lunch. The thought of getting caught sneaking out made Alex nauseous. But as soon as she had read the note, Jasper disappeared from the window. Alex checked the clock – it was only a few minutes before one.

Moments later, the class was dismissed and the rest of the students headed to the lunch hall. Alex quietly snuck off in the other direction, towards the double doors which led out to the school gate. She loitered there, trying to look casual. She needed the corridor clear so she could make a break across the car park without any teachers or students asking questions.

There were a few opportunities, but at each one she hesitated until someone came, and the moment passed. The bell rang to signal the hour and, as if it was a sign, Alex ran, pushing through the doors and emerging into the damp brightness of the car park. Jasper stood under a large umbrella, leaning against the gate.

He lifted the umbrella as she approached. He smiled, though it looked strained. Without saying anything, they walked quickly along the pavement towards the high street. It was busy with lunchtime traffic, men and women dressed in suits, some eating as they strolled and others looking down at their phones.

After walking along the high street for several minutes, Jasper turned sharply down an alleyway between a corner shop and a greasy-spoon café. They stepped past overflowing bins, and the sour smell of rotting food made Alex's stomach turn. Once they were halfway down the alley, where the light was dim and the noise of the road distant, Jasper stopped. He was muttering words under his breath that Alex couldn't make out.

'Jasper, what is this all about?' She looked around uncertainly. 'Why did you bring me *here*?'

He didn't seem to hear her, just began to pace back and forth.

'Jasper!' She grabbed him by the shoulders to steady him. 'You need to tell me what's going on.'

Face on, she could see the way fear had taken over his features, flaring his nostrils, widening his eyes and causing him to chew the inside of his cheek.

'I've broken all the rules, already,' he said, seemingly more to himself than her. 'Why stop now?'

'What rules?' Alex asked.

'They found out,' said Jasper. 'They know everything.'

'*Who* found out *what*?' Alex said, urgently. The tone of Jasper's voice frightened her. She had never seen him behaving like this before – or *anyone* behaving like this, for that matter. Jasper didn't usually worry about breaking rules. The boy she knew was carefree and quick to laugh. But maybe that was exactly the problem. Maybe Alex didn't know Jasper that well at all – not really.

'They're going to take me back,' he said, 'but I had to talk to you first. You were right. I've been lying to you. We're friends and friends don't do that.'

We're friends. Despite her worry, Alex felt a warm glow at those words.

'Listen carefully,' Jasper continued in a whisper. 'I'm not here because my parents moved here. I'm not even from Scotland. I'm here because of *you*, Alex.'

She gave a small, humourless laugh.

'I know this sounds crazy. But, please, we don't have long.'

Alex dropped her smile and adopted the most serious look she could.

'They sent me here to watch over you,' Jasper went on, 'to protect you and stop any of the Tourists from getting too close. Except . . . it was *me* who got too close.'

In the darkness of the alleyway Jasper looked slightly wild. And he wasn't making any sense. Perhaps if they went home, dried off and had a cup of tea everything would be all right again. 'Jasper, let's go home and talk to Uncle Henry—'

'There's no time!' Rainwater dripped from his hair and rolled down his cheeks. 'They're coming to take—'

Jasper's voice stopped dead. His eyes focused on something over Alex's shoulder. She turned to follow his gaze.

There was a woman standing at the end of the alleyway. Her hair was the colour of squid ink and fell neatly down her back. Her face was sharply angled, with cheekbones that looked as though they were cut from rock. She was wearing a long dark-gold dress. In the dim light, Alex could just make out a clear crystal brooch pinned above her heart.

Jasper stumbled backwards.

'It is time to go, Jasper.' The woman's voice was deep, authoritative. She held out a hand towards Jasper.

'The rules aren't fair,' said Jasper. 'If I just tell her—'

'The rules are there to protect us,' the woman said, calmly. 'They protect Alex too, remember. To break them puts us all in terrible danger. That's why there must be punishment for those who do so. You have no choice now but to accept the consequences of your reckless actions.'

Alex flinched at the word *punishment*. She was surprised to hear the woman speak her own name. She had the sense of watching the scene from afar, as if it were a television programme. The woman did not meet Alex's eyes when she spoke; her gaze remained locked on Jasper, her hand still outstretched.

'Come now, Jasper,' the woman said. 'Time to face the music.'

Jasper's shoulders sank. He turned his back to the woman and leaned in close to Alex.

'I have to go,' he whispered. 'I don't know what's going to happen to me now. But one way or another I'll see you again, I promise.'

'Jasper!' screamed the woman. 'Now!' Gone was any trace of calm. Her eyes shone with fury. Alex saw fear on Jasper's face and she shivered.

'You don't have to go with her, Jasper. Please don't go!'

'Bye, Alex.' He wrapped his arms tight around her shoulders in a hug. Then he turned and ran. He reached the woman and took her waiting hand in his own.

'Stand back!' the woman shouted to Alex, ducking her head in a small bow. As she raised her head again, her gaze caught Alex's for one short moment, then fell away. It was just long enough for Alex to notice the look in her eyes. This time it wasn't anger she saw – it was fear.

With her free hand, the woman unpinned the brooch carefully from her chest and held it in in the centre of her palm. The crystal began to spin. It spun faster and faster, until all Alex could see was a blur of blinding, white light illuminating the brick walls of the alley.

Alex shielded her face with her hands. There was a rumbling sensation deep in her heart, the kind you get when standing too close to a speaker. The rubbish on the floor began to tremble around her and started to inch towards Jasper and the woman. Looking from behind her hands, Alex saw a cylinder of light emerging from the crystal, twisting away down the alley like a tunnel. Now Alex's own body was being pulled towards it too, and she had to fight to stay on her feet. Still holding hands, Jasper and the woman were dragged towards the tunnel, twisting through the spiral of light, getting further and further away, until they disappeared from view. Alex was momentarily lifted off her feet as the light gave a final, blindingly bright flicker.

As quickly as the light appeared, it vanished, and Alex fell backwards on to the hard ground, alone in the dark alley.

CHAPTER SIX

Midnight Reading

All the way home, Alex saw bright white light whenever she blinked. It was imprinted on to the back of her eyelids, just as dirt from the alleyway stained her trousers. At the end of every road she expected to see Jasper, smiling at the practical joke he had pulled, bursting to reveal how he'd tricked her.

But Jasper did not appear. Nobody so much as gave her a second look as she stumbled in the direction of home. She was desperate to tell someone what had happened, but there were no friendly faces who might listen to her story. Besides, she knew well enough that nobody would believe her. There was only one person in the world who would and she needed to see him urgently.

Fortunately, Uncle Henry was always easy to find. As

she entered the darkness of the living room, she heard her uncle muttering to himself under his breath. The curtains were drawn and the air stale. He was furiously tapping on his laptop keyboard as if in a trance. Alex waited a few moments for him to look up, but he didn't notice her. In a small voice she said, 'Uncle Henry?'

'Alex, dear, when did you get here?' His face morphed from surprise, to happiness, to concern in a matter of seconds. 'Oh, blimey! Have you been rolling in dirt?'

'Uncle Henry, you won't believe what happened,' she began, pacing the width of the living room. 'There was a woman . . . and she came and took Jasper. They vanished into thin air . . .'

'Alex, calm down,' said Uncle Henry, standing. 'Speak slowly. What happened? Jasper went where with whom?'

'That's exactly the point, Uncle Henry! I don't know. A woman came and said Jasper had to go with her. They disappeared through some kind of tunnel. Except it wasn't a normal tunnel at all, it was like it was made of light . . . and it was so bright it hurt my eyes . . . everything was sucked into it like a magnet . . . and then it disappeared as if nothing happened . . . and Jasper was gone.'

'Alex,' Uncle Henry replied. 'I'm afraid I don't understand a word of what you're saying. If this is some kind of joke you know I never understand them.'

'It's not a joke, I promise,' Alex said, tears beginning to prick. 'It happened just as I said. Jasper is gone and I think he's in trouble. You have to believe me.'

'Of course I believe you. Don't doubt that for a second.' Uncle Henry's face had a look of deepest concern. 'I'm just trying to process what you're saying. Because people don't *disappear* through tunnels. They always come out *somewhere*.'

'But that's what happened! She kidnapped him!' Alex was nearly frantic.

Uncle Henry looked thoughtful. 'This woman, could she have been his mother do you think? Or an aunt or sister perhaps? There must be a logical explanation for what happened.'

'No, no, no. I'm positive she wasn't. She was unlike anyone I've seen before. And the way she looked at him . . . so fierce, angry . . . and at me, like she was almost frightened.' Alex shuddered as she remembered the cold look in the woman's eyes. 'I know Jasper is in real trouble. In danger! He needs our help, Uncle Henry. And this time I don't think logic is the answer.'

Uncle Henry looked at her for a long time. His expression was confused, kind but ever so slightly changed. He was more like an adult, like a regular father, than he ever had been before. He put his palm to her forehead and snapped it back as if he'd touched a hot kettle.

'You're overheating' he said, softly. 'Why don't you have a lie down for a moment and I'll phone the school to see what I can find out about Jasper. They must have his mother's phone number in their records.'

Alex understood this was Uncle Henry's way of trying to help. He was trying to diagnose her in the only way he knew how, like she was a computer. Getting her to go to sleep was his way of turning her off and on again and hoping that would make everything better.

But sleep was the last thing Alex wanted to do. Her mind was working faster than ever before, running over the events in the alleyway on a continuous loop. She spluttered words of protest as Uncle Henry shepherded her towards her bedroom.

'That's it, lie down,' said Uncle Henry. He kissed her on her forehead and pulled the covers up to her chin. 'Have a good rest, my dear,' he said, closing the curtains to block out the daylight.

With a last, worried look, Uncle Henry backed out of the room. Alex lay on her bed staring at the ceiling. There was a knot deep inside her belly that tightened every time she thought of her uncle. It was anger, she realised with surprise. Why did he always have to be so logical? Couldn't he just accept that what had happened to her today was unexplainable?

Deep down, she knew her uncle was doing his best. If she hadn't seen what happened in the alleyway with her own two eyes, she would have reacted the same way. But in that moment, it didn't make her feel any less cross . . . or lonely.

In the darkness of the room, Alex lost track of the hours. She heard the gentle hum of Uncle Henry's voice from the kitchen and strained to make out his words. His tone was steady and warm, as if relieved by what the person on the phone had told him. For all her efforts not to, she must have fallen asleep, because the next thing she knew she woke with a jerk.

Her throat was dry as toast and her limbs stiff. Alex rose from bed and tiptoed to the window, peeling back the curtain. Outside the sky was black and almost starless. All the lights in the houses down the street were off so she knew it must be the middle of the night. Carefully, she opened her bedroom door.

The house was silent and shadowy. It felt like a different place at night, the light of streetlamps outside casting a yellow tinge over everything. In the kitchen Alex poured herself a glass of milk. She sipped it, leaning against the fridge. What was she going to do? Jasper was in trouble and she had to help him. That much she knew for sure. But in order to do that, she had to make sense of what had happened in the alleyway. It was no good wasting time being sad or angry. She could mope and whine until morning, but that wouldn't help her find Jasper. She had to approach the problem like a scientist.

Think, think, Alex said to herself. A scientist starts with observation. The problem was, what she'd observed in the alleyway defied the laws of physics as she knew them. It looked like Jasper had vanished into thin air. And yet that was impossible. A human being is made up of billions and billions of atoms. And those atoms couldn't have just ceased to exist. At least, if her understanding of physics was correct they couldn't have. So, what had happened to the billions of atoms that made up Jasper?

Alex didn't know. But *not knowing* never stops a great scientist. Great scientists revel in the unknown; they use every tool in the scientific box in their search for answers. And when they reach the edge of their knowledge, they turn to research. That's what Alex needed to do. She had to find out everything she could about the laws of physics until she came up with a proper hypothesis for what had happened.

She had to consult her uncle's books.

Alex walked to the living room, flicked on the light and stood, neck craned upwards, in front of the large bookcase. Books were stuffed into every available space and spilled out on to the floor beside it in wobbly stacks. The biggest of the stacks was almost as tall as Alex, with spines stuck out at all angles like a Jenga tower.

One wrong move and the books would tumble, surely waking up her uncle. Carefully, one by one, she extracted the physics books. The stack swayed from side to side but miraculously didn't fall.

Alex climbed into her uncle's chair and spread open a book in her lap. The pages were filled with very small writing, words she couldn't understand and numbers accompanied by odd symbols she'd never seen before. She flicked through the chapters, not quite knowing what she was looking for. When she finished that book, she put it aside and moved on to the next. And then the next.

Reading at such speed gave her a headache. Her eyelids drooped and her head bobbed with exhaustion. She was almost ready to give up. To put the books away and slink back to bed, defeated. And that's when she saw it.

It was near the end of a thin book with a navy-blue cover. A small black-and-white picture made her stop, her hand frozen on the page.

'That's it!' she whispered.

The name of the chapter was printed in large letters above the image:

TUNNELS THROUGH TIME

CHAPTER SEVEN

Robo-Chick

Alex read the chapter over and over. She didn't understand most of what she read; in fact, it made her head spin horribly. But it was the picture she couldn't stop looking at. It looked exactly like what she had seen in the alleyway. A tunnel of bright white light.

Time travel. The words filled her with amazement. According to the author of the book, some scientists believed that light could be used to bend the very fabric of the universe, to form a kind of bridge or tunnel from one time to another. The problem was, nobody had come close to figuring out exactly how to do it. But Alex knew what she'd seen in the alleyway. Jasper had been pulled through a tunnel exactly like the one pictured in the book.

On the one hand, it sounded impossible. On the

other, it was entirely logical. Her uncle had said that people don't just disappear. They must come out somewhere. And according to the book, he was right. Jasper hadn't disappeared into thin air; he had travelled through time. As a scientist, reviewing all the evidence, Alex determined it was the only sensible hypothesis.

But if Jasper had travelled in time, *when* had he gone? In the alleyway, she remembered him saying that he was 'going back'. Did that mean *he* was from another time? That would explain why he was always so reluctant to talk about his past. And why there had been something a bit different about him. Could he really have come from the past? Or the future? The thought was equal parts exciting and overwhelming.

Alex closed her eyes. In her mind, she ran over what had happened in the alleyway yet again. *They sent me here to watch over you* . . . Why would Jasper need to watch over her? *To stop any of the tourists from getting too close* . . . Alex had no idea what he meant by tourists. Or why tourists would want to be anywhere near her.

She thought about the way the woman in the alleyway looked at her. Nobody had ever looked at her like that before. It wasn't anything like the doting way Uncle Henry looked at her. Or the exasperated type of look she got from teachers. Or the way the other children looked at her, as though she was invisible. There had been no humour or warmth in her eyes, like there was in Jasper's. No, the look she had given Alex was a baffling combination of menace and fear. *The rules are there to protect us . . .* she had said. *They protect Alex too, remember.*

How had the woman known her name? Alex couldn't imagine what kind of rules she had meant. She only knew that Jasper was going to be punished for breaking them. And Alex couldn't let that happen.

When the clock's hour hand hit eight, Uncle Henry stumbled into the living room in his chequered dressing gown, waking Alex, who had fallen asleep curled up in her uncle's chair. She was still wearing her school uniform from the day before.

'You're up and dressed early,' Uncle Henry said, yawning widely. He looked at her carefully, searching her face for a sign of yesterday's upset. 'How are you feeling?'

'Better, thank you,' she replied, relieved he hadn't realised she'd been up most of the night.

'Great,' he said, beaming. 'I spoke to the school yesterday afternoon. They confirmed my suspicion that the lady you saw was, in fact, Jasper's mother. A tall lady with dark hair, yes?' When Alex nodded, he continued. 'Well, Mrs Wright says that the lady, his mother, dropped Jasper off at school on his first day. They didn't have her telephone number on file, unfortunately. Seems that her phone was broken the day he joined the school, which is awfully careless if you ask me. And I suspect the tunnel of light you saw them walk into had something to do with being overtired. Our eyes can play all sorts of tricks on us when we need a good night's sleep. But there you are, nothing to worry about. I'm sure you'll see Jasper today at school and he'll be right as rain.'

'Thanks, Uncle Henry,' Alex said. She was dying to tell him about what had really happened in the alleyway. Nobody in the world would be more excited to learn about time travel – or more worried about Jasper. And yet she knew that without him having seen what she had it would be impossible for him to understand.

Before saying another word to him about it, Alex needed more evidence. She would go straight to the school library and take out all the physics books she could carry from there. Once she had more proof, then she would talk to her uncle. Alex pushed the book with the tunnel picture up her jumper – in case she needed it to help explain to the librarian what she was looking for – while her uncle ambled into the kitchen and poked his head into the fridge to retrieve the milk.

'So! Today's the big day.'

'What?' she asked.

'Your project, of course. Robo-Chick!'

Alex had forgotten all about the school science fair. She had worked for weeks on her project, a robotic chicken made out of baked bean tins and old school calculators. It could walk around and peck the ground as well as doing complicated sums on demand.

'Oh, yes.' She tried to sound calm but enthusiastic. 'I forgot.'

'You forgot?' Uncle Henry looked aghast. 'Don't let Robo-Chick hear you say that.'

He passed her a small cat box. Through the metal door, she saw the green glare of Robo-Chick's eyes, the silver shine of her beak.

'I must say, she's quite the handsome specimen. But be careful she doesn't get too close to the other students.' Henry rubbed a long scratch on his palm which had only just start to heal. 'She's a brilliant invention, no doubt, but she has a vicious temper.'

Alex spooned cornflakes into her mouth as quickly as she could. Then she brushed her teeth, fixed her hair and set off for school at pace, the book still tucked up her jumper and the cat box in hand.

'Good luck!' Uncle Henry shouted as she sped out of the front door.

When she arrived at school, Alex headed straight for the library. She was halfway there when her scowling head teacher appeared out of nowhere.

'Where are *you* going in such a hurry?' said Mrs Wright coldly.

Alex mumbled something to her shoes about going to the library.

'The library?' Mrs Wright repeated. 'I don't think so. You should be getting yourself set up for the science fair. There's no time for larking around in the library. Now go on. Straight to the gymnasium. I trust you know the way there by now.'

With a frustrated sigh, Alex turned around. Given the look on Mrs Wright's face her only option was to do what she was told. The minute the science fair was over, Alex promised herself, she'd go straight to the library, no matter what her head teacher had to say about it.

When she arrived in the school gym, several of her classmates were already setting up their projects. In one corner there was a table with a number of glass beakers filled with thick yellow slime. The slime seemed to be moving within the beakers, like it was about to jump right out on to the floor and slither away. On the next table was a papier-mâché volcano. A worried looking boy poured a clear liquid into the mouth of the volcano and leaped out the way as it began to froth angrily with thick red lava.

Alex found a table across the room, safely away from the slime and volcano. On the floor beside her table, she built a small enclosure for Robo-Chick using custard tins she'd taken from the school canteen. She carefully unhooked the door of the cat basket and hopped out of the enclosure.

For a moment nothing happened, then Robo-Chick burst out of the cage. Her beak creaked open and snapped shut a few times as her green eyes surveyed the new surroundings. Alex thought she had better test her out with a few easy sums.

'OK, Robo-Chick. What's five plus two?'

Robo-Chick immediately stopped pecking the ground. Her head snapped upwards sharply, beak opening slowly. She gave a long, sharp squawk which echoed around the gym and caused everyone to turn around. This was followed by six more equally shrill squawks, before her beak snapped shut and she returned to aggressively pecking at the floor.

Alex should have been pleased with her work. It had taken her hours and hours to perfect and had resulted in several peck-wounds in her shins. But as the judging panel of teachers approached, she was so preoccupied with thoughts of time travel she could barely muster enough enthusiasm to explain her invention. Despite her somewhat lacklustre presentation, her teachers were very excited when Robo-Chick managed to work out the square root of sixteen. Excitement was replaced by anger however when her beak snapped shut on Mrs Wright's fingers. In Alex's defence, she had warned Mrs Wright not to get too close.

As soon as they moved on to assess other projects, Alex took out the physics book and turned to the chapter on time travel. She read it for the twentieth time, hoping something would jump out at her that explained everything.

Just then, something across the room caught her attention. It was at the large gym window that looked on to the playground. There were four faces staring through the glass; a man, a woman and two young children. They were wearing matching blue baseball caps and looking straight at her. As soon as they spotted Alex watching, they dived out of sight.

Alex stared at the empty window. She looked

around to see if anyone else had noticed. Nobody had. *Tourists,* she thought. In the alleyway, Jasper had said he was protecting her against tourists. Could this be what he meant? She'd always had strange people popping up at various points in her life to stare at her, and she'd assumed that kind of thing happened to everyone. But what if that wasn't the case? What if these strange people had something to do with *her* specifically? And something to do with why Jasper was sent to protect her? If that was the case, then maybe – hopefully – they could tell her where he was.

Alex saw the tops of four blue caps rise above the window ledge very briefly and disappear again. She chewed the inside of her mouth. She wanted to march straight outside and confront the family at the window. But Alex was paralysed by unanswered questions. What if they weren't tourists here to spy on her? What if they were just a normal family and had nothing at all to do with Jasper? They would think she was completely mad. Or – if they *were* tourists – they could be dangerous. What if they tried to kidnap her, the way the lady in the alleyway had taken Jasper?

What if . . . what if . . . what if . . . Alex's stomach churned with question marks. To confront the people at the window was a huge risk. Alex wanted more time to think, to come up with a plan. But time was of the essence. Jasper was in serious danger. She would have to be brave. She had to act now.

'Right.' Alex put the book on her chair. It was only going to slow her down. For the first time in her life she ignored the voice in her head that was telling her to be careful. She needed a distraction, something to stop the teachers noticing her leave without permission. At that moment, Robo-Chick began furiously pecking one of the tins at the edge of her enclosure.

'Aha!'

With her shoe, Alex nudged the custard tin out of Robo-Chick's path. The robot stopped pecking for a moment, as if shocked at her new-found freedom. Her tin legs took one mechanical step, then another. She seemed to be working out where to go first. Her green eyes shone in the direction of Mrs Wright and she set off, at surprising speed for a mechanical chicken.

She pecked the ankles of every person in her path, causing shrieks of alarm to ring out in the school gym. Soon everyone was scattering out of her way.

Alex took her chance. She half-ran through the crowd towards the door that led out on to the playground. With one last look back to check that no one was watching, she slipped outside.

Ahead of her, she could see the family running across the playground. 'Hey!' she shouted. 'Stop! Please! I want to ask you a few questions.'

They looked back in alarm. The man picked up the smallest child and they ran, disappearing through the school gates and on to the road. Alex followed as fast as she could. Turning on to the street, she skidded to a stop.

There, pulled up by the side of the road, was a large double-decker coach like the one she had seen on the first day of school. The family hurriedly climbed on board. Alex ducked behind a bush as the man poked his head back out of the door, looking from side to side. Seeing no one, his face relaxed into a look of relief and he signalled to the coach driver that the coast was clear.

'She noticed us, but I think we managed to get away.' Alex heard the man say. 'We checked and there was no sign of the boy with her.'

'He must have been taken back to our time, then,' the driver replied, pausing for a moment. 'Come on, we better be on our way.'

Alex's heart thumped loudly. *Were they talking about Jasper?* She couldn't let the coach drive away. She needed answers.

She peeked from behind the bush. Piled up on the pavement were several bags which must have belonged to the family in the blue hats. The driver emerged from the door and stepped off the coach. He unlocked the luggage compartment and leaned inside. His bottom stuck out in the air as he rummaged around.

What would Jasper do? Alex thought. *He would get on the coach,* came the reply.

She knew it was true. What was it he had said about coming to her party? *Act first and think later.* But Alex couldn't do that. She couldn't . . .

Her legs were moving before she knew what was happening. She darted towards the rear wheel of the coach. When she got there, she stood as still as she could, her back flat to the vehicle, peeking around the corner where the driver was rearranging the luggage inside the coach. After a few seconds, the driver surfaced, muttering to himself. Alex held her breath. He turned back to the luggage on the pavement. While he tried to balance as many bags as possible in his arms, Alex tiptoed along the length of the coach and climbed into the luggage compartment. Crawling to a dark corner in the depths of the coach, she lay very still.

The driver, oblivious to what had just happened,

threw a rucksack hard in her direction. It skimmed the top of her head and landed with a thump on her feet. Alex squeaked and the driver paused for a moment. He leaned in closer, looking right towards her.

'Blimmin' rodents,' he mumbled, then tossed the rest of the bags inside one by one.

With two hands the driver heaved the door downwards, abruptly shutting out the sounds and light of the outside world. For the second time in two days, Alex was alone and scared in darkness, with only the sound of her heartbeat for company.

CHAPTER EIGHT

The Coach Station

From within the darkness, the rumble of the engine began. The coach shuddered as the driver lifted the handbrake. A moment later, Alex sensed they were moving. At first, as they drove, she tried to keep track of where they were going. A left here, a right there. But it wasn't long before she was hopelessly confused. *Was that a left or a right? Did we go through the roundabout, or past the park?*

They turned a sharp corner and the suitcases zoomed from one side of the compartment to the other. Alex rolled alongside them, her landing cushioned by a plump duffle bag. Recovering from the impact, she pulled herself on to the bag like it was a surfboard and gripped its handles. The coach vibrated furiously, making everything around her shiver and her teeth chatter together. Eventually, she gave up guessing where they were. All she knew was they were now a long way from Murford. Getting further away with every minute. And there was nothing in the world she could do about it.

As the initial rush of adrenaline began to fade, it was quickly replaced by worry. Alex couldn't quite believe what she'd done. Normally, she was so cautious. Life had always felt safer that way. Now she had set herself on a course into the complete unknown. And that was terrifying.

Despite her worry, the warmth of the engine was making her drowsy. She settled her head on the duffle bag and closed her eyes. In the darkness, it was hard to keep track of time. *Has an hour passed*, she wondered as she drifted off to sleep, *or maybe two?*

Whichever it was, Alex was soon awoken with a sudden lurch. While she'd been dozing, the coach had picked up speed and was now shaking violently. Suitcases rose from the ground and crashed around in the air like they were in a spin cycle of a washing machine. Alex soared helplessly with them, her arms and legs flailing. She was too shocked to feel afraid. Her whole body tensed for the impact to come. She rose higher and crashed back to the floor. Up and down. Up and down. Over and over. Again and again and again.

Then – just as Alex thought it might never end – everything stopped.

Not only stopped but froze. It was as if someone had pressed pause. Bags hung suspended in the air. An escaped frisbee was fixed inches from her nose. Alex clung to the duffle bag, caught in the air as if surfing a wave. It felt like she was moving both forwards and backwards at the same time – like she was caught in a rift between two forces. Alex had just enough time to think how weird the feeling was before she fell back down to the floor with a thump. She lay there, her head spinning, as the vibrations slowly softened. With one final heave forwards, the bus stopped.

Alex breathed hard. Her ears were ringing. Her body ached. The elastic band keeping her sprout in place had come loose, leaving her hair a wild tangle. She took a quick inventory of her limbs. Left leg, right leg, both arms: all present and correct. Bruised all over, but nothing broken. She sighed with relief. Even Uncle Henry would have some questions if she came home limping. *If you get home at all*, sneered a horrible little voice in her head.

Pulling herself up on to her elbows, Alex listened carefully. Somebody – the driver, it must have been – was speaking over a microphone above. Creaks and footsteps indicated that passengers were preparing to get off. It wouldn't be long before they'd be collecting their bags. Scrambling on to her hands and knees she searched desperately in the darkness for the door handle to get out. But, of course, she found no such thing. Luggage compartments don't tend to have handles on the inside. There was nothing she could do except wait.

She hugged her knees and counted the seconds. One . . . two . . . three . . . four . . . five . . . Before she reached six, the floor beneath her tilted with a sudden quiver. Alex was shifted to the side. The driver had opened the coach doors.

Now she could hear the driver's voice on the other side of the metal door. Alex readied herself. In seconds, she would be discovered. A key turned inside the lock, and then the door lifted slowly and daylight flooded in. Alex squinted. The driver's head was turned towards someone Alex couldn't see.

'If Robert is late again, tell him I'm not covering for him . . .' The driver adjusted his belt with one hand. 'I've worked overtime every week this month. You wouldn't *believe* the excuses I've heard from that guy.'

Directly in front of her was the escaped frisbee. In a moment of inspiration, Alex picked it up and crawled towards the light as quietly and quickly as she could. She threw her legs out of the compartment. There was no room for error – she would need to get the angle exactly right. Just as the driver started to turn back towards her, she hurled the frisbee so it curled in a perfect arc towards him. It hit the back of his left shoulder and ricocheted in the opposite direction.

'Oi!' He turned around angrily to his left, looking for the culprit. 'Was that you, Robert? Come on, man, show yourself!'

While he was distracted, Alex sprung out of the bus. She was running before her feet touched the ground. She didn't have time to look where she was running to – she was too busy looking down at her feet and willing them to go faster. It was no surprise, then, that she soon came to a crashing stop.

At first, she thought it was a very solid tree that had sent her flying backwards on to her bottom. But looking up, she realised it was in fact a person.

'Blimey, kiddo,' the person grumbled fiercely. 'You're in a rush, aren't you?'

Alex almost swallowed her tongue. A square-jawed woman loomed over her. She was the most intimidating person Alex had ever seen, with broad shoulders and a pair of muscular arms crossed at her middle. Arched, bushy eyebrows hung steeply over her nose, making her look very much like a disapproving owl. Her face was the kind an artist might carve out of stone, with hard bones and deep lines that only come from a lifetime of frowning.

The woman placed her hands on her hips. 'Are you going to lie there all day? I prefer standing myself, but each to their own.' She gave a chesty laugh that soon became a fit of coughing. 'Oh, come on now. Up! There are rats around here bigger than you.' She reached down and pulled Alex to her feet as if she were made of feathers.

Now that she was upright, Alex looked properly at her surroundings for the first time. And what Alex saw made her stomach lurch.

They were in some sort of hall. The ceiling was glass and domed high above like a cathedral. The floor, what she could see of it, was made of shining marble. People rushed by in all directions. Alex had never seen so many people in one place, or so many with such peculiar clothes. A couple of moustached men walked past deep in conversation, dressed in linen shirts with huge lace collars and baggy breeches, as if they'd walked off the set of a Shakespeare play. They must be actors, Alex thought, struggling for a rational explanation. Then there was a group of five middle-aged women, all wearing flared trousers and floral kimono tops. One of the women carried a lava lamp and another wobbled in a towering pair of platform boots. They were making peace signs with their fingers at everyone they passed.

Alex turned wildly from left to right. Everywhere she looked she saw more people outfitted in what seemed like fancy dress costumes. The more she saw the more confused she became.

'What . . . what is this place?' she asked nobody in particular.

'The coach station, dearie,' said the woman. 'Haven't you been here before? It's a strange place, that's for sure. The finest place in the world for people-watching, though.'

The coach station. Sure enough, when Alex looked behind her, she saw rows and rows of white double-decker coaches. Beside the closest one, people were collecting their luggage from the driver, who was still rubbing his shoulder and looking around with a sour look.

'Were you on that coach?' the woman asked. 'Your outfit is very good, really tremendous. Most Tourists go way overboard with what they wear. They try to blend in with what they *think* people wore on their holidays, based on old travel brochures and photos people posted of themselves online. As if any of that reflected real life! But your outfit is beautifully researched. Very authentic.'

Alex glanced down at herself doubtfully. You would have to be very odd to think her school uniform was *tremendous*. Though 'very odd' might not be too far from the truth, Alex thought, as she took in what the woman herself was wearing: a hooded green gown that fell in pleats to her ankles and had baggy batwing sleeves. Poking out from the bottom of the gown were two neon pink jelly sandals.

'What coach station is this? Where are—' Alex stopped dead. A group of people wearing sun hats and beach sarongs were hurrying across the marble floor. Tourists. Just like the sort of people who had turned up throughout her life without explanation. They chatted excitedly and pulled bulging suitcases in the direction of the coaches.

'More tourists!' Alex whispered. So, this was where they came from, wherever *this* was. That didn't explain, though, what they were doing travelling to Murford. Or why Jasper thought he needed to protect Alex from them.

Watching them bundle towards the coaches, Alex thought that the tourists couldn't have looked more harmless. There was nothing particularly threatening about people wearing open-toed sandals and khaki shorts. But then again, Jasper certainly seemed to think they were dangerous. Maybe she should watch them from a distance. On the other hand, they might know something about where Jasper was. 'Who are all those people? Where are they going?' she asked.

'Where?' scoffed the woman, scratching the fine hairs on her chin. 'Don't you mean *when*? When are they going?'

'*When* are they going?' Alex repeated, slowly. *Time travel*. The words resounded in her head. *Don't get carried away,* she told herself. After all, it was one thing to suspect time travel was possible and quite another to have those suspicions confirmed. 'But that doesn't make grammatical sense.'

'If you say so,' replied the woman coolly. 'Shouldn't you be getting back to your family? They'll be worried, I'm sure. And I have things to be getting on with, other than getting grammar lessons from a child that is.' She looked anxiously around. 'Besides, I have a Time Guard on my tail today so I shouldn't stay in one place too long. I'd finally managed to lose him when I bumped into you but it won't be long before he catches up.'

Alex felt suddenly very odd. The sun shone brightly through the glass ceiling above, drawing beads of sweat from her temples. She had a strong desire to be back among people she knew, even those classmates who ignored her or called her names. The thought of their company seemed almost comforting right now. Plus, if she didn't get back soon, Mrs Wright was going to be furious with her.

'Do you know where I can find the ticket office?' she asked the woman. 'I need to get on a coach straight back home. It can't be too far – not more than a few towns away.' Even as she said it, Alex wasn't convinced. She knew there was no coach station like this anywhere near Murford.

The woman's eyebrow hair bristled. 'You won't find any coaches to take you home here, I'm afraid. This isn't that kind of station.'

'Not that kind of station?' Alex squeaked.

'These coaches only travel to the past.'

Alex's mouth dropped open. It didn't matter a jot that she had thought Jasper might have travelled through time. Having actually travelled through time herself was quite a different matter entirely. Could it really be true?

'Queen Victoria!' bellowed a man behind her, holding an umbrella high above his head. 'Queen Victoria! Those on the Queen Victoria experience, please follow me now. And ladies, please, if you feel like you're going to faint tell somebody in your party straight away.'

At his back shuffled a flock of men and women. The women all looked pained, probably because the long, colourful dresses they wore cinched their waists to the width of a pencil. Their hair styles were quite ridiculous too; tight curls piled high on top of their heads. Alex watched them inch elegantly after the man with the umbrella, wondering how on earth they were managing to breathe.

Alex looked back at the woman, who was now peering at Alex as if her eye was a telescope. 'Do I know you, child? You look very familiar to me, but I can't place you. Have we met before? Perhaps you were one of my students once. But surely you are too young.'

Alex stepped backwards instinctively. The woman leaned on her tiptoes, close enough for Alex to notice she smelled of peppermint and dust. Behind her walked a group of men and women wearing puffy-sleeved dresses and tweed suits with bowler hats.

'Why are those people dressed like that?' Alex said, rubbing her temples, still trying to put all the details together.

'That group there?' replied the woman, casually. 'I believe they're going on a trip to 1892 to see the esteemed lawyer Cornelia Sorabji, lucky things. She was a real marvel. Helped countless people in her lifetime. You definitely wouldn't want to come up against *her* in an argument.'

'The Queen Victoria experience . . . a trip to 1892 . . .' mumbled Alex frantically. 'Is this place a museum? Or a theme park? Yes, that would make sense.'

'Girl, stop babbling. I've told you already, this is a coach station, which you can see plainly with your own two eyes. Why, you came here on a coach yourself. I saw you.'

'Well . . . that's the thing,' Alex began, hesitantly. 'I *did* come here on a coach – but I was hiding in the luggage compartment. I snuck in while the driver wasn't looking. You wouldn't believe how bumpy it was.'

The woman looked like Alex had doused her in icy water.

'You . . . you came in the luggage compartment?' she spluttered. 'Child! You don't mean . . . you don't mean to say that you are a stowaway? A stowaway . . . from *the past*?'

The woman's face quivered like a blancmange. She looked at Alex as one would an escaped lion, partly fascinated and partly terrified.

'You'll have to go back at once,' she said. 'Before anyone realises what has happened—'

Alex jumped on the spot. 'Jasper *did* travel through time, just as it said in the book. And that means this really is the future,' she said wonderingly. 'What year is it?'

'The year? It's the year 2100.'

'2100!' Alex repeated, her hands pressed to her head. She'd travelled *eighty years* into the future. 'I can't believe it!'

The woman took her arm. 'We'll get you on to the next coach back to your own time and nobody needs to know anything.'

Alex stared at her. 'I'm not going anywhere,' she said. 'Not yet!'

' "Not yet?" Child, you don't know what you are saying! Time Tourism is a wonderful thing, no doubt about that, but it can be very dangerous in the wrong hands. The Time Minister sets strict rules for its use. And even stricter punishments for breaking them.'

Rules. Jasper had broken the rules, and that was why he had to leave Murford. 'What kind of rules?' Alex said. 'And who's the Time Minister?'

'Who's the Time Minister!' The woman gazed at her, horror-struck. 'Only the most important person on the planet. The Time Minister was the first to unlock the mysteries of Time Travel. Made all this possible. Established the set of ten rules, called Time Law, which ensure that everyone stays safe. And one of the most important rules is – do not meddle with the past. You can imagine how messy that could get. By sneaking on to that coach, you could change the course of history. You must go back at once.'

Alex shook her head firmly. 'No. I need to find my friend. He's here somewhere, I'm sure of it.'

'Another stowaway? There can't be. Here? But how can you be sure?'

'I overheard the coach driver saying he'd been brought here before I climbed on board.'

Oh, goodness me, goodness me!' said the woman, more to herself than to Alex. 'What have you stumbled across now, Gertrude? Typical, that's what it is. It's like

Mother used to say. You always seem to walk right into trouble and can't help but stop for a chat.'

'Gertrude,' said Alex. 'It's nice to meet you. I'm Alex. I don't want to cause you any problems. But I'm not going on any coach until I've found my friend Jasper. And that's that.'

There was a silence between them, as both stared defiantly into the other's eyes. Seconds later, the large lady's shoulders slumped, and she gave a tremendous sigh.

'It's Gerty Grabble, if you must know. Friends, where I find them, call me Gerty.'

'Well Gerty, thank you for your help so far, but you don't need to worry. I'll be fine on my own.'

'Will you indeed?' Gerty sighed heavily. 'That only shows how little you understand. A child from the past cannot simply get by in a city like this. Besides, the Time Guards don't take kindly to rule breakers. If they find out about your little trip there will be trouble.'

Alex's mouth went very dry. She didn't like the sound of the Time Guards. The thought of being chased by them around a strange, futuristic city filled her with dread. As for finding Jasper, she didn't even know where to start. 'If you'll help me, Gerty, I promise I'll go back home on the first available coach once I find my friend. I just need to make sure he's OK.'

'Absolutely not! No, no, no. You ask too much of me. If anyone ever found out, I'd be sent before the Time Minister. Why, it wouldn't be worth the risk.'

Alex nodded miserably. If only she had something to offer Gerty in exchange for her help. Reaching feebly into her pockets, she pulled out a handful of coins, barely five pounds worth, and her mobile phone, which had long run out of battery.

'I haven't anything to offer you,' she said. 'Unless you want some change and an old phone. Or my watch, I guess.' Alex held out her wrist, letting the light shine across the watch's glass face.

All traces of anxiety on Gerty's face disappeared and she made a cooing sound.

'Goodness me! A watch is a rare artefact indeed. Watches have been out of production for decades. It's a wonder you weren't detected by the Time Guards – they strictly control goods passing through time. Can I just hold it a minute? I collect such precious things from the past, you see, and watches are a personal favourite of mine—'

'It's yours. If you help me find Jasper.'

Gerty gazed longingly at the watch, looked anxiously

around the station, then looked at the watch again. She seemed to be having an argument with herself.

'And I could help you,' said Alex. 'In any way I can. I'm good at making things,' she went on, 'and taking things apart too. I can remember Pi up to one hundred digits . . . and . . . and . . . I have double-jointed thumbs.'

Alex added this last point a little desperately. A hint of a smile formed on Gerty's face.

'Having a kid around for a while wouldn't be the worst thing in the world, I suppose,' Gerty mused. 'This place is crawling with Time Guards today. They're good at keeping themselves hidden, but I know they're here. Perhaps if they see us together, they'll think I'm your mother or something . . . that we're simply going on holiday. You could help me today. Keep the Time Guards from seeing what I'm up to. Yes, yes,' she muttered, 'that could get them off my back, at least for a little while.'

'. . . *and* don't forget the watch,' said Alex, temptingly.

Gerty gave a low growl under her breath. 'OK, OK. You can stop with the sales pitch. I'll do it. But only because I'm in a tight spot today. Don't get any crazy ideas that I'm a nice lady, or a pushover. If you slow me down at all, you'll have to go. And be warned. Before we look for your friend, there's a little bit of work I need to do first here in the station. Some . . . *not entirely legal work* that I don't want the Time Guards to know about. If you get in my way, or cause me any problems, you'll be booted on to the very next coach.'

Gerty stared down, eyebrows raised, at Alex, who nodded vigorously. 'Well, then. I can't promise we'll find your friend. But we'll give it a shot. You have yourself a deal.'

CHAPTER NINE

Taking Care of Business

Gerty tunnelled through the crowd with ease, occasionally elbowing someone in the ribs or treading on their feet in the process. Alex followed as quickly as she could in her wake, murmuring apologies, embarrassed by her new companion's unruly behaviour but also quite impressed. *She can certainly look after herself – and me, hopefully,* Alex thought, watching Gerty bulldoze her way across the hall. *I just hope she'll keep her promise about helping me find Jasper too.*

'Typical,' snapped Gerty when they got stuck behind a particularly slow group. 'Why do Time Tourists always have to move so slowly? Just because *they* are on holiday, doesn't mean the rest of us want to move at a glacial pace. The Time Minister should make it illegal to dawdle.'

Alex nodded, but she would have quite liked to slow down so she could take everything in properly. It was odd to think that every single person in the station was from the future. That the world she saw around her wasn't the one she'd woken up in that morning. Alex would have thought that after travelling through time she'd feel different in some important way. But she felt exactly the same as she always did – except, of course, for the many bruises.

Soon the crowd started to thin and Alex and Gerty emerged into a small clearing in the middle of the hall where Time Tourists, dressed in every kind of outfit imaginable, were gathered in groups. They were all standing with their heads tilted upwards as though looking at something. Without warning, Gerty came to a halt and Alex almost hurtled into her for the second time. Gerty was also staring upwards at what looked to Alex like thin air.

'Aha!' Gerty's eyes scanned from left to right. 'An associate of mine is about to arrive at the station. We made a deal to meet as soon as he arrives. He has some . . . little gifts for me. After that, there are a few more associates of mine that we need to meet, and then we'll set to work finding your friend. Won't take too long, don't worry.'

Alex looked up at the empty space that Gerty was staring at, then back at Gerty. She wondered once again whether her new friend was quite sane.

'OK, but . . . er . . . what exactly are you looking at up there, Gerty?'

'The timetable. Up there.'

Alex glanced back at the nothingness.

'Oh, I forgot – you won't be able to see it. You probably think we're all staring at nothing.' Gerty erupted into crackled laughter. 'That up there is the station's timetable. It will look like empty space to you, probably, but the rest of us can see information about all the comings and goings here. Although right now it's showing an advert for shaving cream.'

Gerty reached for something in her coat pockets and then handed Alex a shiny black object, roughly the shape of a lightbulb with a short metal handle. 'Here, take this this. It's called a holomorph. Look through it and you – only you – will be able to see what I can see.'

Alex held the holomorph upwards in front of her eyes and saw a cluster of speckled lights start to whirl within the black glass. The next second, high above her head, appeared a beautiful, three-dimensional antique clock. Its face was a pale gold colour that shimmered in the daylight, and a pair of intricately designed black hands twitched across its face. Alex was lost in admiration. Out of nowhere, words began to dance across the bottom of the clock.

Hello Gerty! the words read, arriving letter-by-letter. *In ten minutes the 10.30 a.m. carriage you are waiting for will arrive at Platform 1066. While you wait, why not stop by Mrs Bassett's Bakery? They have a fresh batch of your favourite brownies – you know, the ones with the white chocolate chips . . .*

For all the books Alex had read, she could never have believed such a thing was possible. She was dying to know how it worked – whether every person in the station was seeing the same golden clock, and how it knew that Gerty was partial to a white chocolate chip brownie.

'I've been trying to cut down on sweet treats recently,' Gerty said wistfully, as if she could read Alex's mind. 'But they certainly don't make it easy.'

'That is *incredible*,' said Alex. 'Do you think I could take a quick look at how it—'

'No time! My associate will be pulling into Platform 1066 any second. We have to get going.'

Gerty pivoted on one foot, face screwed up at the empty air above her, as though looking for something.

Then, with a determined nod of her head, she set off in a quick march.

'This way to Platform 1066!'

They turned into a passageway that led to a long tunnel. Along the way, Alex held the holomorph up to the walls in case there was more to see. Sure enough, springing to life as if from nowhere, was an advert for shampoo which, she saw with disbelief, featured Gerty herself. Except it didn't look exactly like Gerty. It was a version of Gerty with considerably cleaner hair and smooth, glowing skin. Pretend-Gerty ran a hand gently through strands of her hair while holding up a bottle of neon purple liquid. Brightly coloured letters danced across the screen. *Chroma-Exploda Haircare will give you a new, totally outrageous hair colour with every single wash . . . flamingo pink, butterfly blue, tree frog green, galaxy gloss, tiger-stripes . . . you name it! Go on, Gerty, treat yourself now!*

Does everyone star in their own adverts these days? How strange if they do, Alex thought. But, then again, the future was a decidedly strange place.

They had almost reached the end of the tunnel when Alex caught a smell that made her cover her nose. It reminded her instantly of a school trip she'd been on to a farm in the countryside. It was the hot, unmistakable, smell of manure.

'Gerty, are there animals here?' asked Alex. She was beginning to think that in this time anything was possible.

'We can't always travel by double-decker coach, can we?' Gerty shouted back. 'How would that go down in the year 1066?'

The tunnel opened out on to a hall just as big as the one Alex had arrived in. But this room seemed like it belonged to a different world altogether. It had an arched wooden-beamed roof with birds circling the eaves above. Instead of marble floors, the ground was well-polished dark wood littered with stacks of straw and the occasional scurry of mice. Most impressive of all was the line of magnificent horses which stretched as far as Alex could see. The horses were tethered in groups of four, some harnessed to modest wooden carts with four iron wheels, and others to larger and grander carriages.

The closest cart was pulled-up next to a set of steps. One by one, passengers were climbing out of the cart and down the steps. Many passengers struggled to reach their legs over the side of the cart because of the thick woollen tunics they wore. One man tripped over his cloak as he disembarked, causing him to cartwheel all the way down the steps. He dusted himself off and started walking along the platform. Alex watched him for a second longer before realising that he was watching her right back.

'Hello, Arthur,' Gerty said warmly as he approached.

'Morning, Gert.' The man grinned, rolling up the sleeves of his tunic. He had a head of shaggy hair that fell to his shoulders and a face full of stubble. Both hair and beard were the colour of autumn leaves.

'What do you have for me today?' asked Gerty.

'Hold your horses,' Arthur replied with a wry smile. 'No "welcome back"? No "how was the journey Arthur"?'

'No time for niceties today. There's a Time Guard on my tail. And I have other business to attend to.'

'Other business, you say.' Arthur peered closely at Alex. She stepped backwards defensively. In her own time adults often behaved strangely around her. She didn't think it would happen in the future too. Perhaps, though, that was adults for you – they never changed.

'What's with the child?' Arthur continued, still eyeing her closely.

'She's helping me today, that's all,' Gerty said.

'She looks kind of familiar, Gert. I just can't put my

finger on why.' He nodded at Alex. 'But where are my manners? The name's Arthur Foxtail. It's a pleasure to meet you.' He frowned thoughtfully. 'Why do I know your face? Have we met before?'

'Ignore her, Arthur,' snapped Gerty. 'And stop stalling. Or perhaps you didn't bring me anything at all?'

'Oh, you know I wouldn't forget you, Gerty old gal,' Arthur said. Looking over his shoulder to check the coast was clear, he led them into a shadowy corner of the platform away from the crowds. When he was satisfied that they weren't being watched, Arthur heaved a hessian sack from his shoulder on to the floor in front of him. He reached into the bag until his arm was buried up to the elbow. Alex leaned closer to get a better look.

Arthur pulled out a shiny, uneven piece of metal. 'This marvellous artefact,' he whispered, 'is a silver penny once owned by William the Conqueror.' He held the coin to the light for a moment before throwing it carelessly back into the bag. 'And, would you believe,' he continued, rummaging once again, and pulling out a long thin object, 'that this whistle, carved bone, was used to create the most beautiful song by the very man himself. I saw him with my own two eyes, heard him play with these two ears.'

Gerty inspected the whistle, rolling it in her hands and holding her eye to the holes in the bone. She swung her arm in an arc and landed a heavy slap on the man's back.

'You've done very well, Arthur. I'll look at the rest myself later. Bravo, sir.' Gerty took the hessian sack and swung it over her shoulder.

'Ahem?' he said expectantly, still steadying himself from the impact of the slap.

'Oh, yes. Don't fret, the money is already in your account.'

He grinned and Alex noticed for the first time that his teeth were a breakfast tea shade of brown. Arthur caught her staring and her face burned hot. She hadn't meant to be so rude.

'I almost forgot.' He reached into his mouth and pulled out a set of fake teeth, similar to ones Alex had once worn as a vampire on Halloween. Behind the fake pair was a perfectly straight, snow-white set of teeth. 'No dentists in 1066, you see.' He winked at Alex. 'I always take my costumes very seriously, down to the last detail.'

'Righty-ho, Arth. We'd better be off. You're only my first stop today.' Alex gave her a look which Gerty pretended not to notice. *So much for it won't take long*, Alex thought.

The three of them walked back down the tunnel on to the main concourse. Alex kept a few paces behind as Arthur recounted stories from his trip, illustrating them with wildly dramatic arm gestures that sent Gerty into fits of croaky laughter. It was hard to believe she was walking with someone who had just been hanging out with William the Conqueror. Alex didn't know much about history – it wasn't her strongest subject – but Alex knew that he was very important and lived a long time ago.

When they arrived at the main concourse, Arthur stopped. 'I'm off. I need to get out of this get-up sharpish.' He scratched his arms and neck. 'The itching is abominable.' He paused for a moment, looking again at Alex. 'You *sure* we haven't met before? I really reckon we have.' She shook her head and he shrugged, before disappearing into a crowd of people wearing tunics like his own.

Alex took the chance to observe her new surroundings again. She wished she had one thousand eyes to take everything in. The coach station was the biggest and most crowded place she'd ever been. The jumble of voices, colours, smells and movement was almost overwhelming. It was nothing like the leafy, calm streets of Murford, which suddenly seemed ever so small. Before then, she hadn't gone fifty miles from her front door. Her uncle didn't like to travel much because he got sick in cars, trains and boats, and was afraid of flying. She wondered what he would have thought about the coach station. As she did, she remembered how far away her uncle now was – in space *and* time – and felt a sharp twinge in her chest.

'Come on, kiddo.' Gerty clapped her hands together. 'Our next appointment is just about to dock. Onwards!'

The coach station was enormous and yet Gerty seemed to know its tunnels and platforms better than most people know their faces. They continued at such a pace that Alex's feet started to feel like they were on a conveyor belt.

'Where are we going now, Gerty?' she shouted at her back. Alex was starting to worry that Gerty didn't really intend to help her after all. Perhaps she'd just seen a way of getting some unpaid assistance in her *not entirely legal work*. 'All the marine platforms are in the basement,' explained Gerty, when they eventually arrived at their next stop.

It wasn't really a platform as such but a gigantic indoor harbour. Sitting majestically in the dark water was a fleet of slender wooden ships. Each ship was the length of a giant oak tree with towering white sails that hung limp in the windless air and a complicated system of ropes.

Gerty left Alex on land and walked out on to one of the pontoons. There she met a man wearing a pair of brown baggy breeches, a dirty looking blouse and a leather jerkin. He had a felt hat which he tipped in greeting. Gerty returned after several minutes carrying another lumpy sack. Before she heaved it on to her free shoulder, Alex saw Gerty slip a sword inside the bag.

'It belonged to a fearsome pirate who lived in the eighteenth century known as Anne Bonny,' explained Gerty in an undertone, seeing Alex's interest. 'To be honest, I'm surprised she didn't chop off his fingers for stealing this. Anne wasn't exactly known for her patience.'

I know how she feels, Alex thought glumly as they set off again. When would they start looking for Jasper?

The next platform they visited looked – almost – ordinary to Alex, not unlike Murford coach station. The walls were red-brick and the air was thick with petrol fumes. Alex found it hard to breathe without coughing. Lined up along the length of the concourse were hundreds of shiny red double-decker buses. Alex remembered seeing buses just like them in an old film she had once watched with Uncle Henry. Their thick black wheels and curved roofs reminded her of ladybirds, as if they might stretch their wings and take flight at any moment.

Once again, Gerty told Alex to stay back while she took care of business. As Alex waited, she studied the queues of people in front of the buses. The women were wearing glamorous coats and shawls. Most wore hats but no two were the same. Some were simple, pancake-shaped berets pinned close to the head. Others were draped in ribbon, beads and felt. And some, which Alex liked the best, resembled small cowboy hats with wide brims and a tail feather on one side.

Gerty, meanwhile, had started talking to a woman along the platform. The woman, like all the others, wore a hat – though hers had a veil that obscured most of her face and Alex noticed that her coat pockets looked full to bursting. Alex quietly shuffled closer to the pair until she was in hearing distance.

'I took it from his ashtray when no one was looking,' the veiled woman was saying. 'He never noticed, just picked up another from his box and started puffing away.'

'I have drawers full of Winston Churchill's half-smoked cigars,' Gerty said dismissively.

The woman smiled. 'Well, if the cigar won't do,

how about this?' She looked from side to side to check the coast was clear, then peeled back her coat to reveal something concealed underneath.

'Flippin' heck. Is that . . .?'

'A sketchbook, yes. One of Churchill's most prized possessions. Taken from his study. He was a keen painter, did you know?'

Gerty suddenly looked very pleased. She took both the cigar and the sketchbook and put them in her sack, shook the woman's hand vigorously and turned to go. Alex quickly pretended to be busy examining the floor.

Gerty was still grinning as she approached Alex. 'Right! That's enough for today, I think. We better get this lot back before there's any trouble.' She dumped one of the sacks into Alex's arms. 'Would you be so kind?'

Alex said, rather desperately, '*Now* can we look for Jasper?'

'Yes, yes. Don't fret. I'm going to help you just as we agreed. We'll go to my place first. It's the best spot in this city to think, to find answers. You'll understand when you see it.'

As they swept through the winding corridors of the station, Alex felt a rising tide of worry. As much as she wanted to get out into the city and find Jasper, leaving the station was a daunting prospect. She'd not been there long, but its walls were a safe barrier to the unknowns of the outside world. More importantly, the coaches were the only way she knew of to get back home. But now she was leaving, and with a stranger. It went against everything she believed in. It was dangerous, risky – something she'd never dream of doing in normal circumstances.

However, these weren't exactly normal circumstances. There was no instruction manual to tell her what to do. Alex had to make it up as she went along. She knew very well that Gerty might not keep her side of the bargain; still, as things were, this was her best shot at finding Jasper.

She wondered whether the teachers at school would have noticed she was missing yet. Whether they'd have told Uncle Henry, who would be sick with worry. Or perhaps time didn't work like that at all. Perhaps her uncle and teachers were exactly where she'd left them, frozen as if someone had pressed pause on a cosmic remote control.

It was no use thinking about it too much. Alex couldn't turn back. She needed to find Jasper and save him from whatever punishment he was facing. She had to make sure he was safe. And when she did, she would ask him all the questions that were circling round her brain so fast it ached. Like what he'd meant in the alleyway about *watching over her*. What all this had to do with the Time Tourists. What Time Travellers were doing in Murford. Why anyone would travel back in time to see her, when she was a complete and utter nobody.

She would find Jasper and the answers to these questions. Then – and only then – she could go home.

CHAPTER TEN

Bits and Bobs

The sun was shining brightly as they stepped outside. Alex paused on the stone steps of the station and blinked several times to bring her vision into focus.

She was looking out at a large courtyard. It was a busy scene, a noisy mess of people going about their business. There was a grand water fountain and benches. There were trees, green-leaved with ash-coloured bark, the very same kind that grew on Murford High Street. A family rushed up the steps to the station, bickering loudly about whose fault it was they were running late. 'Did you really have to spend *thirty-four minutes* in the shower? Thirty-four minutes!' shrieked the mother to a teenager who dragged her feet. The benches, the trees, the bickering – these things were reassuringly familiar. It might have seemed, at first glance, that the future was just the same as Alex's own time. That, despite the passing of years, nothing much had really changed. And yet, as her eyes adjusted to the new light, Alex saw that some things were very different.

Impossibly tall buildings surrounded her, leaving only a thin strip of milky-blue sky high above. It was a bit like standing on the floor of a rainforest – or at least how Alex imagined that would feel – if ancient trees had been replaced with glass and metal towers. Alex craned her neck, trying to take it all in. She felt, suddenly, very small indeed, as if not only had she travelled in time, but had somehow shrunk in the process too. This was surely a world built for giants, rather than for people. How could she possibly find Jasper in such a place? It would be like one ant finding another in the Amazon. Alex began to sway on her feet.

'Come on,' said Gerty, marching past her. 'If we linger too long, there's a chance we'll be followed.'

Alex hurried down the steps after Gerty. Until now, she hadn't given a second thought to how they might get to Gerty's place. When she'd imagined the future – something she and Uncle Henry often liked to do – she'd thought hopefully of hovercars and silver robots. But there were no robots marching through the courtyard.

No hovercars zooming through the sky, either. She looked around, imagining floating trains, teleportation pods, flying taxis.

'How will we get to yours, Gerty?'

'We'll walk.'

'Walk?'

'It isn't far. Keep close and don't draw any attention to yourself. OK?'

Alex nodded. Strangers had always stared at her no matter how much she wanted to be invisible, so the last thing she would do was *try* to draw attention to herself. Especially not now, when so much depended on her blending in.

They made their way quickly on to a wide street. On either side stood glass buildings in every imaginable shape – some were slender and others bulbous, some had roof gardens and trees sprouting from every floor, others were so tall they disappeared into cloud. Sitting far below the glass towers was the occasional row of stone buildings, like the kind that was found in Alex's own time. Even though they looked more ordinary to her, they were still far grander than any buildings in Murford. Along the road, oddly-dressed people drifted in both directions with vacant looks in their eyes. It was an expression Alex recognised from Uncle Henry when he was playing his video games. Following a hunch, she held up the holomorph Gerty had given her and looked through it at the buildings.

Just like in the station, three-dimensional images appeared out of nowhere. Across the length and breadth of one of the tallest towers, Alex saw a gigantic advert for peanut butter. On another, a smiling woman who looked like Gerty but with impossibly white teeth whirled in circles wearing a beautiful dress that changed colour with every turn. Every single glass building – and they were surrounded by them – featured an advert for something or other. It puzzled her how Gerty managed to walk straight amidst so much distraction. How could anybody concentrate on where they were going with a giant peanut butter jar dancing right in front of their eyes?

As they walked, Alex's shoulder burned under the weight of the hessian sack.

'Gerty, can I ask you something?' Alex caught up to her march, adopting her most innocent-sounding voice. 'The whistles and cigars and stuff. They're all taken from people in the past?'

'Yes, of course.'

Alex's eyebrows furrowed.

'Yes, child?'

'Well, it's just . . . does that mean . . . are these things all stolen?'

Gerty raised her nose in the air. 'Stolen? Well, that depends on your definition. I consider myself an archaeologist, a collector. I am *not* a thief.'

'But those things aren't yours and you've taken them.'

'If it weren't for me these objects would have been lost in time. I collect them so they can be enjoyed for ever. Some would say I am doing a valuable service to the great thinkers of the past, by allowing their legacy to live on.'

Alex wasn't convinced. 'Don't those supposedly great thinkers ever notice their stuff is gone?'

'Oh, no, no, no. We only take things they wouldn't miss too much. Mostly we take ordinary objects that would have otherwise been discarded or given away. A handkerchief or bedside lamp, that kind of thing. Nothing that would arouse suspicion in the Time Guards, or change the course of history. Anyway, you can swipe something right from under a person's nose and most of the time they'll come up with some story or other to explain its disappearance. Normally they blame a loved one for moving it or start thinking they're going slightly mad.'

Gerty suddenly turned and Alex followed her on to a quiet street of dusty red-brick buildings standing like doll's houses against the surrounding towers. Alex felt instantly more at home; at first glance, the place looked not too dissimilar to Murford High Street, with little shops and canopies over the doors and streetlamps dotted on either side of the road. Signs on the buildings contained words like *Café* and *Ladies Fashion* and *Bank*. Except, when she looked closer, Alex realised that every single building on the street was boarded up, abandoned, and covered in faded and half-finished graffiti, as if even vandals had long ago given up on the place. It gave her the unnerving feeling of walking through a ghost town. And it dawned on Alex for the first time that, though it might feel like she'd landed on a different planet, it was the same world she'd just left, only decades into the future.

About halfway down the street, Gerty came to a stop before a set of glass doors. The frontage of the enormous building was boarded up, and above the entrance was a faded sign with the words WANDLE & SWISH written in elegantly slanted writing.

Gerty heaved the sack down from her shoulder. 'Here we are.'

She waved her arm politely to say *after you*. But

Alex didn't move an inch. She had no intention of venturing inside. It looked like the place might collapse at any moment.

'You live *here*?'

'Yes.'

'Why *here*?'

'Well, kiddo, it's not easy these days to find somewhere large enough to keep all my bits and bobs. Wandle & Swish used to be a very fancy department store. One of the most popular stores on the street actually. When most of the shops around here closed years ago, buildings like this were left empty. It'll be knocked down and replaced with housing or a gym at some point, I'm sure. But for now, it's all mine. The authorities haven't twigged what I'm using it for or there'd be trouble.'

Gerty pushed the door open without using a key. She stepped across the threshold and through a set of ancient-looking security gates designed to catch shoplifters. Alex followed behind, thinking that she should be wearing a hard hat and high-visibility jacket.

The room they entered was enormous. The walls and floor were painted white that had browned and peeled with age. The ceiling was high with exposed pipes and beams. All around, mannequins lay in degrees of nudity; some had been partially eaten by moths while others were missing entire limbs. The ground was littered with broken tables and clothes hangers. Even in its sad, empty state, Alex could imagine how the place must have once looked, filled with shoppers searching for bargains.

At the centre of the room there was a staircase. 'I keep my collection on the second floor,' said Gerty, 'away from prying eyes.'

Alex swallowed hard. She followed Gerty up the steps. She caught the musky scent of dust and mildew. The smell reminded her of an antique shop she'd once visited with Uncle Henry while looking for an old game console he wanted to buy. The antique shop had been stuffed full of weird and wonderful objects and Alex had been scared to move in case she broke something. Now the same smell was growing thicker in her nose and throat. And as she approached the top step and walked out on to the landing, Alex took a loud, dust-filled intake of breath.

What she saw was like the antique shop except one hundred times larger. Shelves from floor to ceiling were crammed full of objects. There were vases and binoculars, vacuum cleaners and microscopes, handkerchiefs and stuffed toys, a jar of hair next to what looked like a waffle maker. Row upon row of glass cabinets displayed glittering necklaces and tiaras. Alex saw meringue-shaped dresses hanging on rails, alongside blue jeans and leather jackets, piles of neatly folded saris in bright colours, coats with padded shoulders and neon ra-ra skirts – even animal skins. She saw a huge display table with every kind of pen you could imagine, from feather quills to biros to felt tips. Stacked precariously next to it were piles of typewriters, desktops, computers, tablets and machines she couldn't even name. She turned, mouth hanging open, to see Gerty already unpacking objects from the hessian sacks.

Gerty carefully placed the cigar into a box containing hundreds of others. One by one she took the rest of the objects and allocated them spaces on shelves or hangers. Alex stood watching her, stunned into silence.

'What do you think, then?' Gerty asked. 'Still think I'm a crook?' She was smiling jokily, but Alex thought she sounded nervous.

'What do I think? I think it's remarkable!'

Gerty beamed. 'I'm glad to hear it.'

'How did you manage it? It must have taken you—'

'Years. Yes, it did.'

'But why?'

'That is a good question. Most things I sell when I

need to. That's how I make a living. I sell through the black market, of course. Items from the past fetch a very good price. Some things, those items I can't bear to part with, I keep here.'

'You said before that the Time Guards – is that what you called them? – don't allow people to take things from the past. How do you get away with it?'

'You do like asking questions, don't you?' Alex's cheeks burned and Gerty smiled at her. 'Don't be embarrassed. It's a wonderful quality in a person. Never lose it. Yes, taking things from the past is strictly forbidden. But my associates and I have ways of getting past the Time Guards' detection.'

Alex was practically bursting to explore. She didn't think she could resist for a minute longer.

'Can I?' She signalled towards the collection.

Gerty chuckled, stepped back and extended an arm. 'Be my guest.'

Alex entered the warren of extraordinary things, hurrying down a path that had been cleared between bookcases and cabinets. In every direction she looked there were curious objects with small white tags attached to them with bits of string. She was so lost in amazement she almost walked into a violin with broken strings that hung from the ceiling. According to the paper tag it had once belonged to Wolfgang Amadeus Mozart. It swayed gently in the air, alongside grandfather clocks and saucepans, ironing boards and chairs.

On a wooden table not far along the path something large and red caught her eye. Alex picked it up with as much care as she could muster. It was a megaphone; the kind people use to speak to large crowds. She turned the paper tag tied loosely around its neck, half expecting to see a price. Instead she read the words in curly handwriting: 'Property of Martin Luther King Jr'. Alex took a sharp breath. Could she really be holding something so historic? She placed it back on the table as if it were made of fine china.

Further along, Alex saw a vast cabinet. It was full of ancient maps and on the shelves beside stood rows of magnificent books. In an open drawer, she saw with amazement, were letters signed by the Indian activist Mahatma Gandhi. In the next drawer were piles of manuscripts. From the bunch, Alex picked up a playscript with the name Ignatius Sancho written across it. According to the paper tag, he was a bestselling British writer and composer born in 1729.

Next, Alex stopped to pick up a thick yellow scroll, which was resting against some dusty hardbacks. As she carefully unfurled it, she marvelled at the paper's strange markings. She read the tag three times to make sure she'd got it right. She was looking at the handwriting of Cleopatra, the last Queen of Egypt.

After the cabinet, Alex came to a towering glass display case. Crammed inside were basketballs and boxing gloves, hockey sticks and netballs, golf clubs and skis. She saw a white sweatband which, according to the tag, had once belonged to tennis player Serena Williams; a yellow cap from the sprinter Usain Bolt; and a wooden skipping rope used by the martial artist Bruce Lee. On the bottom shelf, her eye was caught by what looked like a very clumpy pair of leather football boots. Alex picked them up for a better look. They were so heavy she almost dropped them as she turned them over to read the tag. According to the writing on it, the boots belonged to King Henry VIII. Alex couldn't believe that the game of football was quite as old as that.

She was putting them carefully back on the shelf when something scratched her leg. She jumped so high her head almost hit the bathtub that was suspended above her. Peering down nervously, she saw a fluffy black pillow sitting at her feet.

'Play nice, Mrs Puff. Don't worry, she's very friendly.' Gerty had appeared behind a pile of rackets in various sizes and shapes. 'Ah, the football boots. Old King Henry was an excellent footballer in his day. You can imagine his temper when we swiped those boots from under his nose. Blamed his wife Anne Boleyn for moving them and . . . well . . . you know what happened there.'

Mrs Puff stretched out her paws and nudged Alex's knee gently with her nose before trotting over to Gerty, tail twitching behind her.

'She's a stowaway, like you,' continued Gerty, picking up the cat. 'Belonged to the mathematician Ada Lovelace. Managed to get a lift to the future along with Ada's letters and notebooks, isn't that right Mrs Puff? Poor woman must have missed her terribly. Didn't stop her doing wonderful things with numbers, though, did it?'

'Oh! I've read about Ada Lovelace before,' said Alex, pleased. 'She was a computer programmer, like my Uncle Henry.'

'She wasn't just *any* computer programmer. She was the first ever.'

Alex looked at the cat in Gerty's arms with new-found admiration. The cat stared back at her with ice-cold yellow eyes. She made a mental note to tell her uncle all about Mrs Puff as soon as she next saw him.

'If you like Ada Lovelace, I have to show you this.' Gerty clapped her hands together excitedly. It was clear she didn't usually have people to show around her collection and was delighted to have such a willing audience. 'Now where did I put it . . .'

She disappeared into the collection and Alex heard several bangs and crashes. Moments later, Gerty reappeared, holding a large grey box. The top was covered with numbered buttons. It looked a bit like an old cash register.

'Ta-da!'

Alex struggled to hide her disappointment. 'That's . . . lovely. What is it?'

Gerty sighed. 'This, child, is a very old calculator. It belonged to Katherine Johnson.'

'Who?'

'She was a mathematician. Her genius for numbers sent rockets into space. She helped send the first people to the moon in 1969.'

'Woah,' breathed Alex, eyes wide.

Gerty chuckled. She put down the calculator. 'Seeing as you like maths, I have to show you this too.' She picked up a magnificent cloak made of colourful patterned silk. 'This once belonged to the great Persian mathematical genius Muhammad ibn Mūsā al-Khwārizmī. He revolutionised mathematics around one and a half thousand years ago. It's because of him we have algebra.' Gerty paused thoughtfully. 'But don't hold that against him.'

'I *love* algebra,' said Alex, honestly.

'Yes, I thought you might. You are a strange child, aren't you?'

Alex nodded sheepishly, staring at her shoes. 'I guess I am. Everyone at school thinks so.'

Gerty smiled down at her. 'Being strange isn't a bad thing at all. Do you know who else was something of a strange child? Her name was Wang Zhenyi and she was born in China in – when was it? – oh yes. In 1768. You couldn't get her nose out of books, or her head out of the stars. And you can bet the other kids in the neighbourhood thought she was weird because of it. She taught herself astronomy and did experiments on solar eclipses that had never been done before. That up there is one of the objects she used in her experiments.' Gerty pointed to a crystal lamp sparkling on a high shelf. 'She was really a marvellous weirdo.'

Alex couldn't help but smile. They continued walking together through the collection, stopping every second step to gaze at wonderful things. Gerty knew about every single object they came across. She stopped to show Alex a slip of paper with swirly black writing, which she said was a lottery ticket owned by the French philosopher Voltaire. 'He worked out a way to rig the lottery results and made an absolute fortune. Lived the rest of his days in luxury as a result. And wrote the odd book of philosophy, of course. Such a naughty boy,' Gerty said, admiringly.

How Gerty managed to fit all this information into her head, Alex had no idea. She didn't seem to tire of Alex's endless questions. And no matter how large or small, every object they came across had a fascinating story. 'What's that?' Alex asked, pointing at a small wooden comb.

Gerty beamed.

'We took that comb from Johannes Gutenberg.' She ran her hand across the smooth side of the wood. 'He was a genius inventor from Germany who came up with a little something called the printing press. His invention allowed books to be printed rather than handwritten for the first time. Can you imagine the wrist ache from handwriting thousands of books? He also had an unbelievably bushy beard, which this comb helped to keep in check. Would you like to give it a try?'

Alex said she would not, thank you.

'Suit yourself,' sniffed Gerty, giving her own hair a quick comb. 'But on the subject of handwriting, let me show you this.' Gerty collected something from a desk that looked like a very long stick. 'This is an ancient pen. It was carved from a reed, the very thick kind of grass you find by rivers. That's what lots of the world used to write with for hundreds of years, you see. This one is special because it belonged to Fatima al-Fihri who founded the world's first university, well over a thousand years ago. Students from all around the world travelled to Morocco to study science, astronomy, music, medicine and more. She loved to learn. You can see how worn down her pen is.'

Alex gave a low whistle under her breath. A great wave of sadness suddenly overcame her. Uncle Henry would love it here. Exploring the collection wasn't nearly as much fun as it would have been with him. Thoughts of her uncle turned quickly to thoughts of Jasper and her sadness transformed into guilt.

'What's wrong?' asked Gerty gently.

'This is all wonderful, really it is,' said Alex. 'But I desperately need to find my friend. And I don't have another minute to waste.'

Gerty nodded. 'Right you are. We've got work to do! But we won't be able to think properly without a good cup of tea. Make yourself comfortable in the chair section and I'll bring us some refreshments.'

Gerty swivelled on her heel and strode off in the opposite direction.

'Wait!' shouted Alex. 'Where's the chair section?'

'Keep going down there until you reach a painting of a dapper young man wearing a top hat . . . ugly thing, really, can't miss it . . . that's when you want to take a sharp left. You'll come across one of Galileo's telescopes, two right turns, and that is the chair section. Take any seat you wish, and I'll meet you there shortly.'

Alex was glad she had a good memory. Otherwise, she would have surely been lost in the collection for ever. Soon she found herself standing amongst a menagerie of thrones, benches, wheelchairs and sofas. It was a bit like being at a restaurant with a huge menu and it took her a long time to make a decision. First, she spread herself out on a long, elegant chaise longue (from the bedroom of Marie Antoinette, according to its tag) but thought she might be in danger of falling asleep. She suddenly felt very, very tired. So, she settled on a wooden rocking chair.

There was a clattering sound and Gerty arrived pushing a trolley containing a teapot and a plate of biscuits.

'Here you are.' Gerty handed over a china teacup. 'Excellent choice of chair! The last person to sit on that chair was one of the world's greatest artists, Frida Kahlo.' Her eyes glistened in the dim light as she perched on to a zigzag-shaped chair made entirely out of mirrored glass. 'This is my favourite chair in the whole collection. It was designed by the architect Zaha Hadid. You slide off, of course, but that only adds to the fun. Isn't it brilliant?' She took a huge gulp of tea and followed it with a deep sigh of satisfaction. 'That's much better. Now, let's get down to the business of finding your friend. Why don't you start by telling me all about him?'

Alex wrapped her hands closely around the hot china. Though the room was warm, she was shivering. At first, she'd been able to ignore the shaking deep in her bones, putting it down to shock and tiredness. But now her teeth chattered so hard it made her brain jangle inside her skull. As she relaxed into the chair, Alex felt like she could fall asleep for a week. She sipped at the tea, enjoying its warmth and sweetness.

She rocked herself gently backwards and forwards in her chair. 'I don't know too much about him, that's the problem. He's always been so secretive.'

'That does makes things tricky,' Gerty said gruffly.

'Is there anything unusual about him that might help us?'

'No,' said Alex. 'Jasper is normal, just like anybody else.' Alex knew this wasn't quite an honest answer; there were many things about Jasper that had been distinctly unusual. For one, he had wanted to be friends with her. But she didn't want to admit to that being a strange thing to desire.

Gerty gave her a hard stare. The silence grew until Alex was compelled to speak. 'Well, I suppose, the clothes he wore were kind of strange.'

Gerty's cheeks twitched, like a cat's whiskers.

'Strange how?'

'Um . . . well he always wore this weird green suit. Not really the kind of thing children wear.'

Gerty held her cup perfectly still. 'A green suit?'

'Yes.'

'Broccoli green? No, wait – more like . . . the colour of peas?' Gerty said urgently, leaning towards Alex, eyes bulging out of their sockets more than ever.

'Yes,' said Alex, rather irritably. Though the tea was restoring her strength, her patience was stretched thin. 'Pea-green. Why does that matter?'

Gerty had put down her cup. Her muscular jaw was firmly clenched.

'What?' Alex said, sharply. She couldn't fathom why Gerty would be concerned about something as trivial as Jasper's dress sense. Why were adults always so preoccupied with the clothes children wore? Did some things never change?

Gerty shook her head sombrely. 'It matters because he was wearing a uniform. A school uniform, in fact.'

Alex sat up with excitement, her exhaustion forgotten. She remembered suddenly that Jasper *had* mentioned his old school. In fact, it was probably the only thing he'd told her about his life before she knew him. He had said how strict it was and how they didn't read books except as ways to learn about the past. How could she have forgotten?

'But that's great! If you know which school he goes to, we can find him.'

'It's not great at all.' Gerty's voice was very low and Alex had to lean closer to hear what she said. 'It's not any old school uniform. It belongs to a very special school called the Time Academy, which trains young people in certain particular skills.'

'What skills?'

'The skills needed to become a Time Guard.'

'A Time Guard?' Alex couldn't help but laugh. 'But Jasper isn't a guard. He's a normal boy.'

Gerty didn't laugh. 'If what you're telling me is correct, that means Jasper is no *normal boy*. And he is in more trouble than you could ever imagine.'

Alex's smile vanished. 'What kind of trouble?'

'The worst kind. Taking things from the past is forbidden. But *talking* to people from the past? Becoming friends with them? It's unthinkable! He'll be expelled for sure. But that's not all. They can send people to prison for *a long time* for this kind of crime.'

A lengthy prison sentence – just for talking to someone. Alex tried to gather her wits. 'What do Time Guards do, exactly?'

'Time Guards protect International Time Law. The coach station is crawling with them, but it can be difficult to spot them in the crowds. Some have the honour of being assigned to historical figures, like Shakespeare or Picasso. Their job is to make sure that those who visit the past – we call them Time Tourists – don't attract too much attention to themselves, or accidentally change history. They are also trained to protect the Time Tourists against the many dangers of the past. That's what your young friend is training to do.'

'He said he was there to protect me,' Alex said slowly. 'Why? Nothing historical or important has ever happened where I'm from.'

'We'd have to ask him. But if the Academy sent him there, they would have had a very good reason. He would have been sent to protect someone important.'

A shiver prickled up the back of Alex's neck. She couldn't believe that what Gerty said was true. Could Jasper really be a Time Guard? He was just a boy, her friend. At the same time his parting words echoed in her mind. *I'm here because of you, Alex.*

Focus on finding Jasper, she told herself. *Don't get carried away.*

Then again ... maybe she *was* famous in the future – although she couldn't imagine what for. She thought about the careers test. Everybody else in her class was destined to be incredible things. Politicians, actors, journalists, lawyers, television presenters. But her paper had been blank. She didn't have a clue who she wanted to be when she grew up. And she was nothing like the remarkable people she'd heard about in Gerty's collection. They were extraordinary. They were born special. Not like her. Alex Nobody.

If the Time Academy had believed she was somebody important, they were mistaken. Perhaps Jasper had gone to the wrong house. Knocked on the wrong door. It was an easy thing to do. The postman delivered the wrong mail to their house all the time. Yes – that must have been what happened. It was the only conclusion that made any sense.

Whatever Jasper's reasons – however mistaken he had been – he had decided to become her friend. And now he was in serious trouble as a result.

'We have to do something, Gerty,' Alex said. 'We can't let Jasper go to prison.'

'And what exactly do you imagine we can do?' Gerty laughed, darkly. 'I'm afraid if Jasper really is a Time Guard there is nothing that can be done. The Academy is under the strictest security protection on the planet.'

Alex wasn't sure whether she believed Gerty. Since starting school, she had learned that people didn't always tell the truth. They weren't reliable like a mathematical formula, where one plus one always equalled two. Sometimes they made things up completely. Sometimes they added one plus one and came out with seven, or fifteen, or twenty-three. The teachers were the worst of all. They often said things in lessons that Alex knew with certainty to be incorrect. Like Mrs Wright telling the class that eating carrots makes you see in the dark, or that crusts make your hair go curly, when Alex knew for a fact neither was true. So she knew not to trust Gerty's every word. Her collection was remarkable, without a doubt, but everything in it had been stolen – which wasn't honest. And there was something about the way Gerty talked about the Time Academy that made Alex suspicious.

'How do you know so much about the Time Academy, Gerty?' she asked.

Gerty looked sheepishly down at her hands. Then, in a small voice, she said, 'Because I used to work at the Academy.'

'What!'

Gerty nodded. 'I was a history teacher there for the best years of my life. That's when my collection began. I started taking the odd thing from the past. I was careful, didn't touch anything important. It was always for the students, to help bring my history lessons to life. But about five years and twenty-three days ago, give or take, the Time Minister decided to fire me because of it. Said that I was breaking Time Law, which of course, I was. And good riddance too. After that, I had to find another way to make a living. That's when my collection grew somewhat . . . and I must admit it's been nice to have a kid around to talk to about all this stuff again.'

'I'm sorry to hear that,' Alex said. Her brain was working at a thousand miles an hour. 'But . . . Gerty, if you worked at the Academy, that means you know what it's like. If anyone would know how to break in, how to get around the security, it would be you! You can help me break in and rescue Jasper before they send him to prison.'

Gerty gave a brief laugh. 'I wish it was that easy.'

'Since when do you care about easy? You fool the Time Guards on a daily basis. Look at all this stuff, Gerty!' Alex circled her arms at the marvellous objects that surrounded them. 'Your collection is proof it can be done.'

'It's not the same thing. Breaking into the Time Academy is practically impossible! The Academy isn't only a school. It's also the location of the Time Minister's office. It's where the most senior and esteemed Time Guards meet to discuss International Time Law, under the guidance of the Time Minister. If the ability to travel in Time was misused, if people were free to use it for any reason they wish, for personal or even political gain, the consequences could be unimaginably disastrous. That's why the Time Minister and Time Law is so important. And, if we're to break into the Academy, as you suggest, we'll have to do it right under the Time Minister's nose.'

Alex paused. 'It does sound impossible,' she replied,

carefully considering everything Gerty had told her. 'But then again, people do impossible things all the time. Like sending people to the moon. Like inventing computers. Like Time Travel! If people from the past can do wonderful things, so can we. This is our chance to do something brilliant. To be part of history, not just to collect it.'

The woman stared at her for a long moment, then gave a wheezy laugh and pulled herself up from the chair. 'You can stop that wheedling. I'll help. I did promise, after all. And I've never needed much convincing to do something risky and utterly foolish.'

Alex charged headfirst at Gerty and flung her arms around her. 'Thank you! Thank you!' she cried.

'I . . . don't . . . do . . . hugs,' said Gerty through gritted teeth. She peeled Alex's arms from around her waist. 'Stop it, before I change my mind. Now, make yourself useful and help me clear away the cups. Then I think it's bedtime for you.'

'But Gerty,' said Alex. 'We need to get started on making a plan . . . right . . . away.' Her last two words were obscured by an enormous yawn.

'I don't think so, somehow. You're tired.'

'I'm really not . . .' It was hard for Alex to argue when her every other word was now a yawn. So, she admitted defeat and helped Gerty put the cups and biscuits on the trolley.

'We'll make a plan first thing, won't we Gerty?' she asked sleepily.

'Yes, yes. First thing.' Gerty gripped the clattering trolley and started pushing it away. 'My mother always said I can't leave trouble alone. Always said it would be my downfall.' She paused. 'Let's hope Mother wasn't right about *that* part. The bed section is in that direction, a little way after the Queen of Sheba's throne. Good night, kiddo!'

Alex's head was heavy on her neck as she walked along the aisle to find the bed section. She chose the first bed she came to, a large four-poster with red and gold curtains, and sunk into its lumpy mattress. It had thick woollen blankets and fluffy pillows. It wasn't long before Alex tumbled into deep sleep, dreaming of bright white tunnels and pirate ships.

CHAPTER ELEVEN

The Plan

The next morning, Alex woke slowly. Blankets wrapped around her body like the walls of an oven, leaving her hot and clammy and confused. She kicked them away and enjoyed the instant relief of cool air. Opening her eyes, she saw through blurry vision an intricate pattern of what looked like shooting stars in the dark wood panels above her head. It was so lovely it took her a few minutes to question why it was there at all. And come to think of it, why was her duvet so heavy? And where was the loose spring in her bed that usually poked her in the shoulder? There was no spring poking her this morning. In fact, the mattress beneath her seemed to be made of straw. Gradually, the events of the previous day came back to her. She wasn't in her own bed. She wasn't even in her own time.

Alex got to her feet with a jump, rubbing the sleep from her eyes. Going to bed in her clothes had left her itchy. Gerty was nowhere to be seen but the air was thick with cooking smells. As if on cue, Alex's stomach grumbled loudly.

There were several paths to choose from and she had no idea which was the right one, so she allowed her nose to lead her. Alex soon came across objects she recognised from yesterday, like the painting of the man in the top hat and the hanging bathtub. The sound of music, deep, melancholic and beautiful, drifted from somewhere close by. She followed the notes until she found the source, a vinyl record player sitting on a small wooden table.

It sat in a space that looked like an improvised kitchen, with a toaster and fridge and towers of tinned food. A plaintive voice was singing now. And, humming along with the record, was Gerty, swaying gently as she laid out breakfast plates. Mrs Puff sat in a chair watching her, the tip of her tail twitching with the song's slow rhythm. Alex watched too, without saying a word, until the record fell silent.

Two slices of toast popped up with a ping. Gerty swivelled around to collect them, saw Alex, and jumped.

'Ohhh!' she gasped. 'Kiddo, you gave me fright.

How long have you been there?' She flushed with embarrassment. 'I should leave the crooning to Billie Holiday, that's for sure.'

'Sorry,' said Alex. She was finding it hard to think of anything else except the hot toast Gerty was now spreading with butter and the pan of scrambled eggs.

'Go on, help yourself,' said Gerty. 'Plenty more where that came from.'

Four rounds of toast later, and three cups of sugary tea, Alex was finally satisfied.

'Don't they feed kids where you come from?' Gerty said, smiling.

Alex wiped buttery crumbs from her lips with the back of her hand.

'Right,' she began, draining the last of her tea. Now her belly was full, there was only one thing on her mind. 'We need to make a plan to break out Jasper.'

Gerty raised her bushy eyebrows expectantly. 'I'm listening.'

Alex hesitated. 'Well I don't exactly have everything figured out yet. But you must know more about the Time Academy than most people, Gerty.'

'Yes, that's true. Though nobody knows it entirely. The Academy always has a degree of mystery. Secrets that it keeps hidden.'

Alex paced back and forth. 'You can't go inside the Time Academy, Gerty, can you? They'll recognise you instantly.'

'Correct.'

Alex paused thoughtfully. 'But they won't recognise *me*.' Gerty opened her mouth to protest. 'No, listen. I'm the right age for a Time Academy student, aren't I? So, what if I go undercover? If I dress up in the green uniform, I'll look the part. If you can help me get inside, I can do the rest. Then I'll find Jasper and break him out, before they lock him up for good.'

Gerty listened, her eyes narrowed. 'It could work,' she admitted. 'It *could*. If you keep your head down and don't attract too much attention to yourself. They'd never expect it, after all. Children so rarely try to break *into* a school. Usually it's the other way around. But where do you imagine you'll get a Time Academy uniform from?'

'Come on, Gerty. Are you telling me you don't have any Time Academy uniforms here? You have *everything*.'

Gerty's mouth twitched with the hint of a smile. 'I might do.'

'I knew it,' said Alex, grinning. 'So, now we need to work out how to get me past security. Are there guard dogs, killer robots, security guards . . . what?'

'Security doesn't work like that in our time. I can explain how it does work, but it will be easier to show you. First things first though, let's find the uniform.'

They left the plates on the table for Mrs Puff to lick clean, which she did enthusiastically. A short walk away was a clothing rail the length of several train carriages with hundreds of different outfits. Most, Gerty explained, were costumes for her associates to wear when travelling to the past.

They walked beside the rail until they reached a line of green. Gerty plunged her arm deep into the clothing rail. 'There they are. Try . . . *this* on for size.' Gerty pulled out a green suit with a shiny waistcoat, identical to the outfit Jasper had worn. Rummaging around on the floor beneath the railing, she found a pair of black boots. 'Put these on too. And I'd better get dressed into a fresh gown, I think.'

Gerty disappeared and Alex quickly dressed in the strange, stiff suit. When Gerty returned a few minutes later, Alex was lacing up her boots.

Gerty was dressed exactly the same as before, in a green gown, as if she hadn't changed clothes at all. Her wardrobe must have been like Uncle Henry's, thought Alex, which was filled with identical-looking baggy T-shirts and jeans. She imagined a clothing rail nearby with hundreds and hundreds of undistinguishable green gowns.

'Oh, yes,' said Gerty, as Alex straightened up. She sounded impressed. 'Don't you look good. Like a real baby Time Guard.'

Alex felt good too. She tucked her hands into the waistcoat and knocked the heels of her boots together. She hated trying on clothes normally – they never felt like they fit her quite right. But wearing the Time Academy uniform made her feel relaxed, comfortable even.

'No time to admire yourself. You might look the part, but there's lots you don't know. Follow me.' Gerty scurried through the collection with the easy determination of a mole through earth. They took a new route but somehow came out at the same staircase where they'd started the day before.

Stepping out of the collection was like emerging from a thick forest; Alex shielded her eyes from the daylight that streamed through windows above. The sudden brightness had a dizzying effect, and so Alex was grateful when Gerty suggested they take a seat on the staircase that led down to the ground floor.

Gerty sat, her hands in the front pocket of her gown, and sighed deeply.

'Before you try to break into the Time Academy, I need to explain something. It's an important part of how the modern world – my world – works. And I believe it will help you rescue Jasper.' She shifted uneasily. 'But it's something nobody from the past – especially no child – should know about. It's against Time Law to tell people from the past secrets about the future. There's no way around it though; you've got to know. But you can't tell another soul. Do you understand what I'm saying?'

Alex nodded. 'I promise,' she said. Aside from Uncle Henry, there wouldn't be anyone to tell anyway. Although it would be fun to see the look on Mrs Wright's face.

'Good. I'm trusting you. And that's unlike me. So here it is.'

Alex shuffled closer to Gerty on the step, wishing she had a pen and paper to take notes. Gerty spoke for several minutes, hardly stopping to breathe. Alex tried her best to keep up, and though she thought of a million questions, she kept quiet and listened.

'So,' she said, when Gerty had finished, taking a deep breath, 'you're saying that there's something in your brain – a computer chip of some kind. Which means you can see and do things I can't?'

Gerty looked relieved. 'Exactly! You've got it in one. Every baby born in the country is given one. A tiny implant no bigger than a grain of rice. It makes our brains work better than they otherwise could.'

'In what ways?'

'In every way! Like the clock in the station. Remember that? The chip in my brain means I can see that without needing the holomorph. And it means the station's timetable is tailored exactly for me. Earlier when I was waiting for Arthur, I didn't need to study a long list of platforms to find out when he was due to arrive. All the information I needed was right there waiting.'

Alex swallowed. What Gerty said was fascinating, unbelievable, exhilarating and deeply strange. She couldn't decide what she thought about it.

'And that's only the beginning,' Gerty went on. 'If I fancied it, I could make everything in the world look blue, as if I was looking through blue glass. Or red, or yellow, whatever I wanted. I can completely block out certain noises, if I'm trying to concentrate for instance. And can measure a distance just by looking at it.'

Alex's eyes wandered up to Gerty's head, half expecting to see wires or a flash of red light in her eyes. A bit like Robo-Chick, perhaps. She saw in Gerty's eyes only the look of kindness that had been there all along. 'Can you feel the chip in there? Does it hurt?'

'Can you feel your brain?' Gerty laughed so hard her eyebrows shook. 'No, I can't feel a thing.'

'Don't you find it weird? Going about your life with bits of metal in your brain?'

'Frankly, I have no idea how you exist without it.'

Alex frowned. This seemed like terrible news. She didn't have a chip in her head that gave her special abilities and everyone else in the country did. Her brain was completely unremarkable. She was powerless.

'I don't stand a chance in that case, do I? My brain doesn't have any powers. I can't see in the dark or search the internet with my mind. The Time Guards will eat me for breakfast.'

'Well, that's where you're wrong,' Gerty said, smiling. 'It might be your greatest advantage.'

'How?' asked Alex.

'Because they won't see you coming. That's how I take things from the past, don't you see? It's not only our brains that have computer chips these days. It's everything, from toasters to toilet seats. They're all connected, which means they can do special things. Take a simple pair of trainers for instance. Having an electronic chip means the trainers can change colour if you want them to. Or they can sense if your toes are getting cold and warm them up. Or make you walk with a bounce. And of course, the chips also make everything trackable, which is used for security reasons . . . But in the past, in your own time, things didn't have special chips. Things were just ordinary.'

'And what's wrong with ordinary?' Alex interrupted. It was her duty, she thought, to defend her own time.

Gerty ignored her. 'The chips are how Time Guards make sure people don't take things from the past. They use special scanners to check that everything brought here by Time Tourists has a chip in it as it should. Anything that doesn't have a chip is immediately confiscated.'

Alex sat up as she suddenly caught on. 'So . . . you trick the scanners?'

'I do indeed. I found a way to hack into their scanners to make objects from the past appear like they have chips belonging to ordinary holiday objects. The Time Guards scan Winston Churchill's cigar, for example, and their scanner tells them it's sun cream. Even huge things like baths and cellos appear on the scanners as beach towels or ear plugs. They could have a quick look to check, of course, but they never do. They trust the scanner more than their own two eyes.'

Alex thought for a moment. 'For people with computer chips in their brain that seems very stupid.'

'It is!' laughed Gerty. 'And the Time Guards at the Academy are exactly the same. The Academy has the tightest cyber security in the world. Everyone who arrives at the school is scanned to make sure they are authorised to enter. There's no need for security guards or guard dogs any more. We're identified by the chips in our brains, you see. They would never imagine someone turning up without a chip. They'd think it was impossible! You're the *only person* in our time who doesn't have one. And right now, that's an excellent thing.'

'If they can't detect me with their scanners, does that mean I could walk straight in?'

'Yes. Perhaps,' Gerty said. 'With a bit of luck, it might work.'

In this strange world, Alex was the odd one out. Again. But for once, it gave her a huge advantage. In a way, it gave her the power of invisibility. 'Say the security system does let me past,' she mused. 'Say I can get inside. Won't they spot me? How will I find Jasper once I'm in?'

'You'll have to be discreet, of course, keep a low profile. But once you're inside the Time Academy it shouldn't be too difficult to go undetected. You might have noticed that people aren't very observant these days. Too distracted by the chips in their brains. And the teachers at the Academy are no exception. Now, as for finding Jasper, it won't be easy. They'll be keeping him locked up somewhere in the Time Academy. I imagine that there will be a tribunal shortly to decide what to do with him.'

Alex gave Gerty a questioning look and Gerty explained.

'Like a kind of court case, but not for regular crimes. It's only for those who've broken Time Law. At the tribunal, his punishment will be deliberated by the Time Minister. Once that happens, I expect he'll be taken straight off to prison. It's a serious crime to break Time Law like he did.' Alex winced, which Gerty ignored. 'You'll need to find out where he is and break him out *before* he's sentenced. After that, it will be too late. Only the Time Minister would be able to pardon him then.'

'Where do you think they'll be keeping him?'

'I don't know for sure. His whereabouts will be classified as top secret, no doubt, but somehow gossip always seems to get out in that place. You should ask the students what they've heard.'

'I'll talk to the students, got it.' Alex paused. 'So

that's it, we have a plan. All that's left now is to actually do it. We better go soon if we want to reach him before his tribunal.'

She was nervous. Everything else aside, going to a new school was scary. She hadn't exactly had the best experience at her own school. And even if she managed to get inside the Time Academy, somebody might still recognise her as an imposter. What would happen if she got caught? Would they throw her into prison with Jasper?

'Gerty,' she said, nervously, 'do you really think this will work? There's a lot that could go wrong.'

To her surprise, Gerty threw back her head with a chesty laugh. 'My trade is the past, kiddo. Ask me anything you like about that. But I've no idea at all about the future. Nobody does. We're strictly forbidden from travelling ahead of our own time. It's possible, of course, but far too dangerous.'

Gerty stood up and hopped down the steps two at a time. 'Nobody in the history of the world has travelled ahead of their own time.' She paused thoughtfully, turned back to Alex and winked. 'Except for you that is.' There was a loud meow from the fluffy black rug sitting on the bottom step. 'Oh, yes, and Mrs Puff.'

CHAPTER TWELVE

Sandcastle by the River

They set off for the Time Academy straight away. Gerty put down a saucer of food for Mrs Puff, who ignored the offering petulantly. The furball weaved between Alex's feet in protest at their departure and mewed loudly as they left through the front door.

Back out on the busy city streets, Alex felt safer than she had done the day before. Yesterday she had been worried that someone would notice that she didn't belong. She hadn't known, then, that everyone was far too absorbed in their own thoughts to notice anyone else. And now that she knew about the computer chips in people's brains, the things she saw made much more sense. People passed her openly talking to themselves. Others glided along the street without seeming to notice their surroundings, robotically dodging obstacles that came across their path.

She didn't need to worry about cars, either; she hadn't seen one since she'd arrived. There weren't even pavements on most of the streets they walked down. Instead, people rode machines that were similar to bicycles, with seats, handlebars and pedals, only they all had glacier-blue frames and shining silver discs in place of wheels. They looked to Alex like they had been carved from ice, the way their glassy frames glistened in the daylight. These bicycles zoomed smoothly along the streets at unbelievable speeds, even though their riders were pedalling slowly and lazily as if going for a Sunday ride. Miraculously, the cyclists weaved amongst pedestrians without crashing into anybody. It was almost as if the bicycles could sense where people were and avoid them. That would have seemed like a silly idea to Alex before she'd arrived in the future, but now she could believe anything was true.

'They're called Cy-cles,' Gerty said.

'Cycles?' replied Alex. 'Like bicycles?'

'No. *Cy*-cles. The Cy stands for cyborg because they connect to our brains. I prefer walking when I can help it, but we'll certainly get there quicker if we use one. And time is of the essence . . .'

Alex couldn't say 'yes please' quickly enough. Gerty said they could take any Cy-cle they found without a rider. And, sure enough, it wasn't long before they came across one parked up against a tree. They had to share; like everything in this city, Gerty explained, the Cy-cle connected to the electronic chips in people's brains to work. It wouldn't move anywhere without one.

Alex thought Gerty looked a very funny sight sitting on the bike, with her green gown almost reaching the pedals. It was a struggle for them both to fit on the saddle, but they did, somehow. Alex clung as tightly as she could on to Gerty's shoulders.

'Are . . . you . . . ready?' Gerty boomed.

'Think so!' squeaked Alex in return.

Before Alex had a chance to be sure, they were off. It was wonderful hurtling down the city streets with the wind in her hair. They zipped around trees and turned corners so sharply her shoulder almost touched the ground. Once, they even did a wheelie to avoid running over a cat. If Alex hadn't known better, she would have thought Gerty was a professional stunt woman.

'How did you do that?' Alex shouted to her, after a particularly impressive jump.

'It's not me, it's the Cy-cle. All I have to do is keep pedalling!'

They turned a corner and Alex could see a river up ahead. The water, Alex noticed, was the brownish colour someone makes when they wash paintbrushes in a bowl. They followed a road along the riverbank, almost keeping up pace with the boats that sped across the surface of the water. On the other side of the river was a jumble of buildings squashed together as tightly as could be. Some looked very old, even to Alex, and others sparkled with newness, like different generations of a large family.

'Look!' shouted Gerty suddenly, pointing across the river. 'The Academy!'

The sun was making it hard for Alex to see what Gerty was pointing at. She shielded her eyes with one hand and squinted until an outline started to take shape.

At first, the outline was all she could see. Then finally it came into focus. Hundreds of windows glittering beneath pointed turrets. Stone walls the colour of sand. She recognised it at once.

It was the Houses of Parliament. Alex had seen it before on the six o'clock news. But never in real life. On the television screen it always seemed so big. And yet beside the gigantic glass buildings of the city, it reminded her of a sandcastle – a particularly impressive one, the kind that would win first place in a national sandcastle competition.

Alex was surprised to realise they were in London. She had never been before, though she suspected she might not have recognised the city even if she had. But – why were they going to the Houses of Parliament?

Without warning, they turned sharply. Alex had to grip Gerty's shoulders hard so as not to fall off. They were halfway across the bridge before Alex knew what was happening.

'Gerty, where are we . . .' Alex began, trailing off mid-sentence. In an instant she had completely forgotten what she was going to ask. Standing high above their heads, with the dignity of a wise old man, was Big Ben.

Slowing down, they approached the end of the bridge. When they came to a stop, Alex was still staring upwards at the clock tower.

'She never gets less wonderful,' said Gerty, in an uncharacteristically soft voice. The loose skin of her neck quivered with emotion. 'Not another school like it in the world.'

'School?' Alex stammered. 'I don't understand.'

'Yes, child. This is the Time Academy.'

'*Here?*'

Gerty smiled, eyes twinkling. 'Where else?'

'But,' Alex began, unsure, 'isn't this where the government meets to make decisions about the country?'

'Oh, yes! It was,' Gerty said, nodding. 'But a long time ago it was decided that maintaining International Time Law took priority over petty government business. And so the politicians moved out and the Time Academy moved in. Quite right too. The government still runs the country, of course. But the Academy looks after the boundless wonders of Time itself. There's no greater responsibility than protecting the past, present and future.'

'They moved out the government for a *school*?'

'Not just *any* school,' replied Gerty, sharply. 'The most prestigious educational facility in the world. When the pupils in this Academy graduate, they will be responsible for protecting not only our future but our past too. Nothing is more important. It was always my dream to teach here, to guide its pupils in this noble calling. Couldn't believe my luck when the Time Minister offered me the job.'

Gerty had gone misty-eyed. Alex stared up at the building. She was looking at the Time Academy, right here, in the building she had known as the Houses of

Parliament. And Jasper was inside. He could be looking out of one of its many glittering windows as they spoke.

'It's not only the Time Academy,' continued Gerty, matter-of-factly. 'The Time Minister's office is here too. At the top there.'

Alex's eyes followed in the direction of Gerty's finger.

'The Time Minister's office is in Big Ben?'

'Big who?' Gerty asked. 'Oh yes, the bell in the tower. It hasn't been called that for decades. These days it's known only as the Time Minister's office.'

Alex stared up at the pearly white face of the clock, admiring the elegant navy-blue hands, the delicate numerals. She would have liked very much to open up the clock tower for a better look, to see what was hiding inside.

'We had better not linger,' said Gerty, looking around carefully. The entrance is over there. Prepare yourself. This could work like a dream. Or there could be serious trouble . . .'

Alex swallowed nervously. They walked around the side of the building until they arrived at an arched wooden door. On either side were stone statues, one of a unicorn and the other of a lion. They made Alex feel even more on edge, with their fierce eyes and snarling mouths.

'Are – are we going in there?' she asked.

'If you want to find your friend, yes we are,' replied Gerty, though she didn't look happy about the prospect either. 'I'll take you as far as the steps, so I can explain how security works. Then you're on your own.' She tapped her foot impatiently. 'Don't just stand there, open the door, girl.'

Very slowly, Alex lifted one of the black wrought iron handles and pushed hard. The door opened with a long creak. Beyond the doorway was darkness. They passed through the archway. What Alex saw as she emerged on the other side took her breath away.

She had thought that the coach station was impressive, but the hall she now stood in was truly incredible. The walls were grey stone. High above their heads, dark wooden beams criss-crossed the width of the ceiling. There was no furniture and the temperature was several degrees colder than it had been outside. At the end of the room, glowing with light, was a huge window. Alex was drawn towards it, as one would be drawn to warmth on a winter's day.

'This is a school,' choked Alex, wrapping her arms around herself. It wasn't in the slightest how Alex thought of a school – places with playgrounds and the lingering smell of gym socks.

One of the most important features of a school that was missing, Alex realised, was the pupils themselves. 'Where are the children?' she asked.

'This is just the entrance,' Gerty said, in a respectful whisper. 'We need to get up *there*.'

Gerty pointed towards a shallow set of stairs at the other side of the hall.

As they crossed the room, Alex had the sensation of following footsteps that had been walked long before she was born. She noticed that Gerty was puffed up to double her usual size, pigeon chested and chin high. When they arrived at the bottom step, she watched as the woman closed her eyes and took a deep breath.

'Are you ready?' she asked, eyebrows deeply furrowed.

When Gerty had mentioned security at the school, Alex had imagined it to be the kind you have at airports – X-ray machines and lots of serious looking people in uniform. There wasn't anybody here that looked like they might be a security guard – not even a reception desk. There was nothing Alex could see to stop them walking up the steps.

'What's the problem?' Alex murmured. 'They're just steps.'

Gerty's eyes flew open with anger. 'Just steps? Do they teach children nothing in your time too? These steps are part of history!' she hissed. 'Countless kings and queens have been crowned on these steps. Many have undergone trial here, including Guy Fawkes himself. Nelson Mandela gave a speech a mere two metres from where you are standing.'

Alex was silenced. She remembered that Gerty had been a history teacher at the Academy. She no doubt knew more about the history of the building than anyone.

Gerty put a hand on Alex's shoulder. 'These steps are not what they seem. Only those that are authorised may climb them. If someone tries to walk up the steps without permission, the chip in their brain will make an excruciatingly loud, skull-scraping noise. No lasting damage they say. But it's not very pleasant at the time . . . or so I've been told.'

Gerty saw Alex's stunned expression and quickly added, 'Don't look so worried. It can't happen to you, silly, you don't have anything in your skull. Except your brain obviously. But you understand now why you have to go up alone. I'll wait for you down here.

When you get inside, talk to some students and find out what you can. As you're in uniform, they shouldn't get suspicious so long as you act naturally.'

That was easier said than done, thought Alex. Seeing her hesitation, Gerty gave Alex a thump on the back and whispered, 'Better get a move on! Go now, go on!'

Alex took a deep breath and ran forwards. She made it up three steps in one leap, tripped and steadied herself. Her eyes were scrunched up tightly in anticipation of the skull-scraping noise Gerty had warned her about.

Nothing. Slowly, Alex opened her eyes. Her head was blissfully free of pain, something she'd never appreciated before. Alex ran up another step, then another. She turned back to see Gerty beaming, two thumbs up, with a look of immense relief on her face. Alex waved goodbye and, with one last look, disappeared up the Time Academy steps.

CHAPTER THIRTEEN

The Time Academy

With soundless footsteps Alex crossed through the arch at the top of the stairs. The first thing she noticed about the corridor on the other side was how cold it was. It was dark too, dimly lit by a row of glowing chandeliers. Draped across the walls were huge paintings, hanging one after the other like windows into the past. Their paint was faded, and the style very old, and yet Alex couldn't help but stop to admire them. She liked the stories they told, stories of magnificent wooden ships, chaotic swordfights and flame-haired queens. She was rather less fond of the frowning stone statues standing guard beside them with their bellies stuck out pompously. They looked to Alex like they might spring to life at any minute and start shouting orders at her.

The corridor led into another extraordinary room. It was round, or to be more precise octagonal, with a golden, domed ceiling and a gigantic sparkling chandelier. Hundreds of statues were carved into the stone walls and red and black tiles covered the floor in intricate patterns. There was so much to take in, Alex's eyes became fuzzy. The hall had the unique smell all old and important places have, a mixture of musty wood and lingering candle smoke. She would have liked to shout as loudly as she could to hear the echo, but it seemed like somewhere you should probably whisper.

This is the Time Academy, thought Alex with a deep breath. She spun around on the spot trying to take it all in. If she'd had a month or two, she might have succeeded in that endeavour. But as things were, time was of the essence. She hadn't come all this way simply to goggle at beautiful architecture; no, she had come to find Jasper.

Alex looked around the room and counted three stone doorways, four including the one she'd entered through. She was deciding which of the three others looked most promising, when she was interrupted by a thunderous noise.

DONG . . . DONG . . . DONG . . .

Her heart skipped a beat, or possibly three. She froze as the great bell completed its sombre count. The silence that followed was short-lived, broken by a new noise – a rumbling sound that grew louder with every second, threatening to shatter the stained-glass windows above. Then, just when Alex was seriously considering whether to turn and run, streams of students burst through the three doorways. They filled the hall in seconds with a vast ocean of green.

It looked at first like complete chaos. But once Alex looked properly, she realised how startlingly well organised it all was. The students marched one by one through the hall in neat criss-crossing lines, like ants at a picnic. Alex was impressed and a bit daunted by their coordination. She wondered whether Jasper was somewhere among the moving green suits. And for one glorious moment she thought she saw a flash of dark sticking-up hair at the other side of the hall. But when he got closer, the boy's head turned to reveal a stranger's face.

As quickly as it had filled, the hall started to empty. Alex knew she had to act fast. She needed to speak to one of the students – without making them suspicious.

Alex scanned the crowds, looking for children who might be in Jasper's class. She caught sight of a line of students about her age, walking in her direction. When they were close enough, she hurried to join them.

This should have been easy in principle. In practice, though, it was a bit like joining the end of a very serious and fast-paced conga line. The girl at the back with brown plaited hair was swinging her arms sharply backwards and forwards like a soldier. Alex was forced to dodge out the way to avoid hard karate-chops to the ribs. This was difficult to do while at the same time keeping up with the quick pace. She broke into a jog as they snaked out the hall. She tried and tried again to catch the attention of the girl with a 'Pssst, pssst!', but the pace was such that conversation was impossible.

They marched through a warren of halls, rooms and corridors, up some staircases and down others, and were soon so deep within the belly of the building that Alex would have found it impossible to retrace her steps. She was relieved when the march started to slow and the girl's swinging arms returned abruptly to her side.

They stopped in front of a mahogany door with the words 'Medicines and Maladies' written in gold letters across it. This was certainly not a subject they had ever studied at school in Murford. Mrs Wright considered anything outside of reading, writing and arithmetic to be frivolous. They'd had woodwork lessons once and all the children had loved them, Alex especially. But to their dismay, the subject was cut when Mrs Wright sat in on a class and deemed it not just frivolous, but '*extraordinarily* frivolous'. Alex was sure that Mrs Wright would think similarly about a subject named 'Medicines and Maladies', which made her even more curious to find out what it was all about.

She didn't need to wait long. The mahogany door swung open and a voice in the classroom shouted for them to 'Come in!'. Alex watched, anxiously, as the students filed inside. Attending lessons wasn't part of her plan. Surely the teacher would immediately realise she wasn't meant to be there, and she'd be found out. Silently, she began to back away down the corridor.

But before she had got more than a few steps, a short man in a green gown with batwing sleeves emerged from the classroom. It was the same outfit that Gerty wore, only without the neon pink jelly sandals. It must have been the teacher's uniform, she thought – Gerty still wore hers even after getting fired. This thought was soon interrupted by the teacher, who was bristling with indignation.

'What are you doing, lingering in the corridor? You are now *fifteen seconds* late for class! May I remind you that lateness is *not* tolerated at this Academy under any circumstances. Those who disrespect the sacredness of Time won't last long here, mark my words! Now, don't dawdle. Come inside and sit down, quickly, quickly!'

Alex had no choice but to do what she was told. She walked into the classroom with her head bowed to obscure her face. She chose a desk right at the back. The classroom had thick green carpet. When she dared to glance up, she saw that at one end, where the teacher stood scowling, was a fireplace and a large desk covered with objects like stethoscopes and surgical masks.

'We're a little late today,' he announced, with a sidelong glance at Alex, 'so let's begin immediately.' Then he frowned. 'Hang on. There's one too many of you. Twenty-two students should attend this lesson, according to the register. But my scanner counts twenty-three occupied desks. That can't be right.'

Alex shifted nervously in her seat. Suddenly she remembered what Gerty had said about people believing their chips more than their own two eyes. She raised her hand nervously.

'I'm new,' she said. 'Did nobody tell you I was joining today?' She closed her eyes and put her finger to her temple, as if she were consulting her brain chip.

'Yes, this class is definitely on my schedule. They must have – umm – not updated the register.'

'No, they did *not* tell me.' The teacher eyed her narrowly. 'Very well. I'll take this up with the schedule coordinator later. Now, where did we leave things? Oh, yes. The ancient Greeks.' Alex exhaled with relief. She couldn't quite believe how easy it had been to convince him. 'They are widely credited,' he continued, 'as having started the field of medicine as we now know it. What's important to remember when visiting ancient Greece is that they believed in something called the four humours. Can anybody tell me what they were?'

A boy raised his hand. 'Yes?' prompted the teacher.

'Blood, phlegm –' there was a groan of disgust – 'black bile and yellow bile.'

'That's right. The ancient Greeks believed that disease was caused by an imbalance of these four humours. This was the basis of medical treatment for thousands of years . . .'

The rest of the lesson was a blur of disgusting facts. Like how doctors in ancient Greece used to taste patients' earwax to diagnose illness. Or how they sometimes applied crocodile dung as sun cream. Every now and then, the teacher pointed to something in empty space that Alex couldn't see, and the class squealed with revulsion. At other times, he told long and rambling stories about his time living in ancient Greece.

'The parties were fantastic, let me tell you,' he said, with a twinkle in his eye. 'I was fortunate enough to be assigned to guard Hippocrates for an entire year. I was fresh out of the Time Academy and what a first assignment that was. Couldn't believe my luck! I still wear my himation sometimes . . . that's a kind of cloth worn draped across the body, which they had back then. I only wear it around the house, when I do cleaning and things. It's incredibly comfortable . . .'

The class sniggered. 'Anyway,' the teacher continued with a cough, 'he was a charming man . . . had quite the ego, but I suppose being the father of modern medicine would make you a bit full of yourself, wouldn't it?'

During a particularly long story about gangrene, Alex seized the opportunity to try once again to talk to the girl with swinging arms who was now sitting beside her, frowning with concentration. She was small with a slight build, though Alex knew from her karate-chop arms she was strong. 'Excuse me,' Alex whispered.

The girl turned her head slightly and whispered back, 'We're not meant to talk in lessons.'

'Sorry!' Alex was relieved to finally get a reply, even

if it wasn't particularly forthcoming. 'I'm new. My name is Alex, what's yours?'

'Meera Shah.'

'Nice to meet you, Meera.'

'You too.'

There was a silence and then Meera whispered, 'He likes to relive the glory days before he got stuck here teaching us. He could be sunning himself in ancient Greece right now, and instead he's talking about crocodile dung.'

Alex smothered a laugh. She was making progress. 'Meera, do you know a boy called Jasper Song? I'm trying to find him.' Meera opened her mouth as if to say something but shut it immediately. The teacher was looking straight at them.

'You can talk through my lesson on gangrene if you want,' he shouted. 'But don't come crying to me when your leg falls off in the Middle Ages!'

After this, Alex was too scared to talk to Meera for the rest of the lesson.

'Next week,' continued the teacher when the lesson came to an end, 'we will be preparing for our upcoming field trip to see the great medical practitioner Mary Seacole. As you should all know, she was a British-Jamaican nurse born in 1805 who used her medical knowledge to treat the poor souls of the Crimean War, among many other accomplishments. You are to all read her autobiography from start to finish for next week's lesson.'

With that, her classmates rose to their feet and started to march towards the door. Alex figured her best bet for now was to stay with them. Everybody in the school moved in groups. If she walked around alone, she would stand out for sure. Besides, she'd almost got somewhere with Meera. She could tell by the look in her eye that she'd known something about Jasper. Alex just needed to try again.

That was easier said than done, however. The next lesson was called Cyber Surveillance. It involved sitting in a circle with their eyes closed, learning how to scan objects with their minds, which made it impossible for Alex to talk to Meera. And without a chip in her brain, Alex had to pretend to scan objects. However, she was so convincing that the class applauded her efforts.

'Very good!' shouted the teacher, a tall woman with long braided hair. Alex had correctly identified a tennis racket as just that (by opening one eye and taking a peek). 'When you graduate as Time Guards,' said the teacher, 'the ability to scan objects with your minds will help you to track down criminals who wish to break Time Law.'

The final lesson of the morning was Language Through Time. This was taught by a young teacher with a high bun. 'To really pass as a native speaker when you travel to the past – to do your job as a Time Guard – you need to know slang,' she explained. 'And today we're going to learn about the 1980s. So, *don't have a cow*, this lesson is going to be *totally awesome*.' Alex had something of a head start in this lesson too, because most of the words they learned were favourites of Uncle Henry. He was always saying that video games were *rad* or shouting the word *ace* when he'd finished a tricky piece of computer coding.

By the time the lesson finished, Alex had learned lots of new 1980s slang to try out on Uncle Henry, but she was still no closer to finding out where Jasper was. She was relieved that it was lunchtime. It would be easier to quiz Meera out of class and away from the gaze of the teachers. And besides, Alex was ravenously hungry.

On their way to the dining hall, Alex took the chance to ask Meera questions about the Time Academy. Meera told her things like how it had over one thousand rooms including its own hairdresser and a fully equipped gym. There was even a swimming pool on the third floor, she said. Apparently, a few years before the roof started leaking and, rather than doing repairs, they turned the whole room into an Olympic-sized pool.

'The building is ancient so nearly everything is broken or leaky,' explained Meera. This was something Alex had already seen with her own two eyes. Most of the walls had large cracks and some of the curtains were half-eaten by moths. Then there were the rats, fat and haughty creatures who sauntered down the corridors like they owned the place and weren't the least bit scared of human children.

The dining hall, as Alex expected, was no regular school canteen. The tables were laid out with white linen tablecloths and silver cutlery. The walls were patterned with flocked green wallpaper and the windows looked out on to the river, giving the impression they were on a docked ship. The room was decorated with hundreds of clocks, every kind imaginable, covering every inch of wall. Grandfather, electric, cuckoo, stopwatch, the list went on. All the clocks seemed to be set to different times too, which meant that every few minutes one of them chimed the hour.

'You've picked a rubbish day to start,' Meera said, as they waited in the lunch queue. 'We're having pottage today. It's a kind of gloopy soup that the

Tudors ate. They like us to try food from history so we're not shocked when we're on an assignment. But anything from before 1800 is almost always dreadful.' Alex saw a boy walk by with what looked like a bowl of steaming glue. 'And later we've got a whole hour of Time Law. Snore! My favourite lesson is Physical Combat because I'm really good at sword fighting. I can take somebody down with one swipe of my arm.'

When they'd collected their food, Alex and Meera took a seat at a table overlooking the river. Looking out at the city beyond, Alex thought of Gerty. She imagined her pacing back and forth, growing impatient, wondering what was taking Alex so long. She opened her mouth to ask Meera about Jasper, when one of the cuckoo clocks above her head sprung into life.

'Why are there so many clocks in here?' she found herself asking.

Meera grinned. 'We made most of them in Clock Club. We build our own clocks from scratch and do repairs on old timekeepers. Last week I got an old grandfather clock to tick again. It's really quite exhilarating. We're always looking for new members, if you fancy it? There are seven of us now so it's really taking off.'

'Yes, pl—' began Alex enthusiastically, before stopping herself. She had to remember that she wasn't really a Time Guard in training. She was only pretending. Her mission was to rescue Jasper and she couldn't forget that for one minute.

'Listen, Meera,' she whispered. 'The friend I mentioned, Jasper Song. Do you know him?'

Meera stopped stirring her pottage. She blinked several times before responding. 'We're not really meant to talk about him.'

'So, you *do* know him?'

'We all know him. Or know *about* him. It's the talk of the Time Academy.' She shrugged. 'But I don't get involved with any of that gossip. It's not my business.'

'I'm not interested in gossip, either,' Alex said firmly. 'I need to talk to him.'

'You won't be able to talk to him. Somebody saw him being taken to Disciplinary when he got back from his special assignment. He's probably still there; at least he will be until his tribunal this afternoon.' Meera resumed eating her soup like the matter was settled. Alex dropped her spoon into hers. It sunk into the grey goop and disappeared with a disgusting slurping sound.

'Disciplinary – how do I find that?' pressed Alex.

Meera frowned. 'You wouldn't want to, trust me.'

'I do! *Please*,' Alex insisted.

'If you really must know,' Meera said with a sigh, 'it's upstairs, past the swimming pool and up the spiral staircase. But you'd have to be crazy to go there willingly. I've never been sent to Disciplinary and I hope I never will.'

Alex was on her feet in a second. Meera looked astonished. 'But you can't go! We're not allowed to wander around the school by ourselves. If you get caught, you'll be in serious—'

Alex was halfway across the room before Meera could say *trouble*. 'He might not be there any more! What about Clock Club?' Meera shouted as Alex manoeuvred around tables towards the door.

Alex didn't hear her. Her face was set in an expression that Uncle Henry knew very well. It was look that said *nothing is going to stop me now*. Not the hardest sum, or the most impossible paradox, or a dining hall full of Time Guards eating Tudor soup.

Hurtling down the corridor, Alex leapfrogged over a family of startled rats who squeaked angrily. She followed the smell of chlorine to the swimming pool, where a canoeing lesson was taking place, ran along it to the other end of the room, and arrived panting at the spiral staircase. She took the stairs in twos and reached, at the top, a corridor that was cold and dimly lit by a row of low-hanging lampshades. Something smelly dripped from the ceiling and on to her head. She hesitated, but the thought of Jasper scared and alone forced her to keep going into the darkness.

The ornate wooden door at the end of the passageway was taller than Alex several times over. She had to stand on her tiptoes to reach the large iron knocker. Sweat gathered at her temples. Meera was right, she thought. She would have to be crazy to knock on a door like this. She needed a plan for what to do on the other side. But there was no time to make one. Jasper could be led off to the tribunal any minute. If she got to him, they could work out what to do together. Like Jasper had said the day he knocked on her front door: act first and think later. And so, knock is exactly what she did.

CHAPTER FOURTEEN
Mr Parrot's Disciplinary

Nothing happened for several seconds. Then, with a loud creak, the handle turned and the door squeaked open.

A face appeared in the narrow opening. In the dim light of the corridor, it was difficult to know whether the face belonged to an old or young man. Alex could tell, however, that it looked exceptionally unkind.

'Well, well, well,' said the man, flatly. 'This is a surprise. Which one of my colleagues sent you?'

'Nobody sent me. I came on my own.'

There was a long pause. 'Came on your own, did you now? How very kind of you to drop by. Do come in.'

A bony hand reached through the door. It grabbed Alex by the waistcoat and yanked her into the room before she could say a word about it. As she recovered her balance, the man swiftly shut the door and took a key from his gown. 'I don't believe we have had the pleasure of meeting before.' He twisted the key in the lock behind her. There wasn't an ounce of pleasure in his voice. 'My name is Mr Parrot. Why don't you and I have a nice chat . . .'

Alex straightened her waistcoat, crossly. Mr Parrot didn't look like the kind of teacher who would be satisfied with a nice chat. In fact, Alex suspected he had his own definition of *nice* altogether. His hair was grey with flecks of black and white, and fuzzy sideburns ran down his cheeks. It gave him the appearance not of a parrot, but of a disgruntled badger.

When Alex looked around she was surprised to realise that they were standing in a library. Not one like the school library in Murford, however, which had only a few chipped shelves and books with soggy corners. This library was magnificent. It was two storeys high with shelves from floor to ceiling stuffed with thousands of books. Squashy red leather armchairs were positioned in cosy corners. It was the kind of place Alex could imagine Jasper curled up in, happily. He'd have worn the same look of contentment that he'd had in her living room the first night they'd met.

The students who sat in the chairs, however, did not

look content. In fact, they looked downright miserable, so miserable you'd have thought they were cleaning toilets, not reading books. One boy was repeatedly pinching himself on the arm and wincing, as if to keep from falling asleep. Alex desperately scanned the room for Jasper, but he was nowhere to be seen. She felt her optimism deflate like a popped balloon.

'Follow me, please,' Mr Parrot sneered.

Alex trailed the man through the library like he was an undertaker at a funeral procession. He seemed to cast a dark shadow over the beautiful space, making it as dreary as a prison. There were rows and rows of bookshelves and Alex checked each one she passed, but there was still no sign of Jasper.

At the far end of the library Mr Parrot stopped at a grand desk and sat ostentatiously in the large leather armchair behind it. He gestured for Alex to sit on the small, uncomfortable-looking wooden chair on the other side of the desk, which she did. Mr Parrot's mouth was set in a line, his eyes permanently half-closed with sarcastic thoughts. He was the kind of person you couldn't imagine smiling even if you tried really hard. The kind who probably had been born a middle-aged man inside and over time had grown to look like one too.

'Right then. Shall we start with your name?' He sounded bored to tears by his own question. He was still holding the key to the room, Alex noticed, turning it over in his fingers.

'Alex,' she said quietly. She said it again, more bravely this time.

'Very good. Now, Alex. Are you going to leave me in suspense? Or will you tell me – why are you here?'

Alex panicked, wishing that before knocking on the door she'd taken a moment to come up with an excuse. 'I – I got lost,' she stuttered.

Mr Parrot gave a sigh that lasted at least ten seconds.

'Lost? My dear, really. You can do better than that. It's the equivalent of telling a teacher that the dog ate your homework. So, I'll ask again. What *were* you up to, wandering around the school alone?'

Alex didn't risk saying anything this time.

'I'll help you out. Was it a dare? Knock on poor Mr Parrot's door and run away. Is that it? You wouldn't be the first to think that was a good wheeze.' He paused for her to reply, and Alex remained silent. She had a feeling that answering his questions would only make him angrier. 'Or perhaps you were trying to visit one of your little criminal friends,' he continued. 'Distract them from their well-earned punishment.' His eyes sparkled with contempt. 'Speak up, or I'll make you read every single book in the philosophy section. Twice! Your brain won't be the same again.'

Alex didn't think this sounded too bad as far as punishments went. In fact, it sounded like quite a nice Tuesday afternoon activity. This thought must have shown on her face, because Mr Parrot's mouth was now the shape of an upside-down crescent moon.

'There are other ways I can get answers, of course. If you refuse to talk, I can always look inside your head myself. The Time Minister doesn't approve of such measures. But it can be our little secret.' Alex felt more frightened than ever before. She gripped the underside of the chair as if it were about to elevate from the floor. Mr Parrot rolled up the sleeves of his gown eagerly.

'Do you know that there is a tribunal today?' he went on. 'A student is most likely going to be expelled from the Time Academy. Thrown in prison for a very long time. The shame is unimaginable.' He shuddered, then scowled at Alex. 'And I don't want to miss being there because I'm stuck dealing with you. So, don't try my patience.'

Alex lifted her head. He was talking about Jasper. Maybe she was in the right place after all. 'Is that student here right now?'

Mr Parrot's eyes narrowed. 'Of course not. We wouldn't let such a criminal lounge around here as if he'd merely given in late homework! He was here for a short time, while we made alternative arrangements. But now he's under lock and key in the basement, guarded by the head teacher. Although not for too much longer; the tribunal begins shortly.'

Alex felt a wave of disappointment. She opened her mouth once, twice, but couldn't find any words. Jasper *had* been here, but she'd missed him. Mr Parrot cracked his fingers and his neck, so loudly Alex felt it in her own bones.

'Which is why I need to determine *your* punishment quickly. Except that you don't seem to want to cooperate. Well, we can't have students gallivanting around the Time Academy without explanation. Oh, no, no, no, no. It poses a risk to the rule of Time itself!' He rose to his feet with sudden enthusiasm. 'I'm satisfied that the head teacher will agree with my decision, even if the Time Minister disapproves. Yes, yes, you give me no other choice. I will look into your brain myself.'

Two girls sitting in armchairs close by sucked air between their teeth. They had stopped reading, or never really started, and clearly had been listening to every word. Their shock made Mr Parrot almost, though not quite, smile.

'I need the device. And then we can get started.' Though he tried to hide it, there was a hint of excitement in his voice, like a child about to try out a new toy. He hastily searched the drawers, pulling things out and throwing them on to the desk with thumps and clanks. 'Where have I left it? Wait right here.'

He disappeared into the depths of the library. Alex tried to force down a rising tide of panic. She couldn't let Mr Parrot try to read her mind. It wouldn't take him long to figure out that she didn't have a chip in her brain to read. From there it was only a hop, skip and a jump to work out that she was from the past. And then Jasper wouldn't be the only one facing a long prison sentence.

Disciplinary had been a dead end. Jasper wasn't there – he was locked up somewhere else guarded by the head teacher. The only thing for it was to get out the library as quickly as she could. Searching the room for a way to escape, Alex's eye was caught by a flash of bronze on the desk. The key to the library. Mr Parrot had left it there by mistake. This was her chance.

Alex checked that the coast was clear. She guessed she only had seconds before he came back. She reached quickly across the desk and grabbed the key. Now all she had to do was leg it towards the door. But there was no time. Mr Parrot was already on his way back across the library, blocking her path to the door. If she tried to make a break for it now, he would get there first. She shoved the key in her pocket and sat hastily back down. All she could do now was wait for the right moment to run.

To her relief, the two girls nearby hadn't noticed her steal the key. They were too busy whispering to each other.

'I can't believe we're going to miss it,' said one girl, her ponytail swishing. 'A student hasn't taken part in a tribunal for years. Apparently, he was *just* about to tell her when Ms Crale arrived. If she hadn't intervened when she did, who knows what would have happened.'

'He's always been strange,' replied the other. 'Has his head permanently stuck in a book. I said that they shouldn't trust him with such an important assignment, but do they ever listen to me? The Time Minister insisted on it being him, apparently. I still can't believe they gave the job to a first year. What did they expect would happen?'

'What do you think they'll do to him?'

'They'll expel him for sure. Send him to prison. Strip him of his Time Licence, probably. Deserves worse if you ask me.'

'And yet nobody did ask you.' Mr Parrot had returned, holding something that looked exactly like a sheet of paper-thin black glass. 'Fortunately, we have much smarter people to make decisions for us.'

He turned towards Alex, looking almost eager. 'All ready to go!'

Alex's fear was overtaken by curiosity. Plus, she needed to stall him somehow. 'You can use that to look in people's brains? How does it work?'

'No point trying to delay things now. Sit still and don't say a word.'

There was nothing else Alex could do. She knew if she tried to run now she'd be caught before she made it to the door. So she did as she was told. Mr Parrot swiped a bony finger at the glass, tongue between his lips in concentration. 'Here we go, here we go! It's starting. Scanning will commence in three . . . two . . . one.'

Mr Parrot eyeballed the glass greedily. He looked at Alex's head, and back again. Nothing happened, as Alex knew it wouldn't. She didn't have a chip in her brain, so there was nothing at all for him to scan. She braced herself, knowing it was only a matter of moments before the truth was discovered.

'Come on!' shouted Mr Parrot. 'Why . . . isn't . . . it . . . working?' He prodded the glass angrily several times, then gave it a shake. He was blaming the scanner, not her. Gerty had been right when she said not having a chip would be her greatest advantage.

'Oh,' he moaned, 'I hate modern technology! This kind of thing never happened in my day. Everything was so much simpler. Girls, come over and help me.' Alex's heart sunk. These girls would surely know how to work the scanner – they'd probably been trained on it in lessons.

The loudest of the two – the one with the ponytail – rolled her eyes and slunk over. She watched him wrestle with the glass, sighing deeply. 'Mr Parrot, you're going to break it if you keep hitting it like that. Hand it over.' The girl snatched it from him. With a delicate stroke she brushed her finger across the screen. He watched over her shoulder.

'Slow down, I can't see what you're doing.'

'It says it can't find a connection with her brain, sir, but that's obviously impossible.'

'No connection? Ludicrous. Give it back.'

'It must be broken.'

'It's brand new!'

'That's what it says, sir.'

'Let me look.'

'No, wait—'

'Now!'

Sulkily, the girl did as she was told. 'But if *it's* not broken, sir,' she said carefully, 'it's got to be something to do with . . . *her*.'

'Her?'

At exactly the same time, they both looked up at Alex.

'What did you say your name was?' Mr Parrot asked Alex suspiciously.

Alex bit her lip. Mr Parrot leaned closer to Alex and she leaned back, trying to evade his glare until her chair was balanced precariously on two legs. He leaned a bit closer. She leaned further back. Then, as chairs on two legs are apt to do, it fell backwards and crashed on to the floor. Pain spread instantly across her bottom. Mr Parrot and the girl peered down at her with blank expressions, too startled to say a word.

Alex clambered to her feet. Every pair of eyes in the room were fixed on her. All reading was abandoned. It was now or never. She made a break for the door.

'Stop!' screamed Mr Parrot, scrambling around his

desk. 'Don't take another step! Don't you know the door's locked?' His eyes were alight with rage. 'You won't be able to get out. Not without the key!'

'Luckily I have it right here,' she shouted, waving it triumphantly.

Mr Parrot gave an anguished cry. 'Give . . . that . . . here!' He charged towards her across the library like a small rhino.

Alex reached the door and slotted the key in the lock. Or at least she tried to. She kept missing. Why did her fingers choose now to behave like they were made of gelatine? Mr Parrot was already halfway across the room. With a long, deep breath, she steadied herself and tried again. This time, the key went in. She turned it and the lock clicked. Slipping through the doorway, she paused to give Mr Parrot a small wave goodbye and quickly shut the door, locking it behind her.

Alex sprinted down corridors with no idea where she was going. A crowd of students leaped aside to let her pass. 'Sorrryyy,' she shouted to them, her face burning hot, lungs wheezing. Eventually she came to a corridor she recognised from earlier with green carpets and panelled walls. If she recalled correctly, as long as she continued along it, she'd soon be back in the room with the golden dome. Alex took the next corner at speed. Then, seeing what waited on the other side, came to an abrupt stop.

Not far ahead, dressed in hooded green gowns, were three teachers deep in discussion. They had their backs to Alex and hadn't noticed her arrival. She retreated speedily around round the corner. They were speaking in whispers but were close enough that she could hear them clearly.

'It's an unprecedented error. What *was* the Time Minister thinking, sending a boy like that on such an important mission?'

The second teacher shook her head seriously. 'It makes a mockery of everything we're trying to achieve. I mean, it's only *Time* we're dealing with here. The entire history of the world as we know it!'

The third teacher nodded enthusiastically. 'Well said!'

Alex crept backwards as quietly as she could. Her palms sweated. Where could she go? Mr Parrot wasn't likely to stay locked in the library for long, and when he escaped, he'd go to straight to the head teacher. They'd discover that she'd stowed away from the past and it would all be over. She wouldn't be able to help Jasper. Would she be sent back right away, she wondered? Or would the Time Minister put her in prison? Maybe she'd be able to see Jasper then. But if she was locked up she'd never see Uncle Henry again. The thought of that made tears gather behind her eyes.

The teachers' voices grew louder. They were heading right for her. That was when she felt it. A groove in the wooden panel behind her back. She was standing in front of a door, she realised with a start. She pushed at it. To Alex's immense relief the wood moved backwards ever so slightly. It was very stiff, but the door was unlocked.

Alex thrust herself against the door. She used all her strength, grunting as she pushed. With an abrupt hollow thump, the door finally gave way and Alex tumbled headfirst into darkness. As quickly as she could, she scrambled to her knees, found the handle and closed the door behind her.

CHAPTER FIFTEEN
The Tribunal

'What is this place?' Alex whispered to the darkness.

She had landed on something spiky and bristly. Was it an animal of some kind – like a hedgehog or a particularly coarse rat? Alex put out her hands to lift herself up and found more of the same. *There's loads of them!* she thought. This was the kind of situation where ordinarily someone might scream and run away as fast as they could. But Alex couldn't make a peep or move a muscle – because, on the other side of the door, with slow and deliberate footsteps, walked the three teachers.

After a few seconds, the footsteps stopped right outside her hiding place. The floorboards beneath the green carpet creaked. She could hear the teachers talking. Alex held her breath. Had they seen her go into the cupboard, or were they just stopping again to chat? The door had been so stiff that it seemed like it hadn't been opened for some time. Maybe, Alex thought hopefully, this room had long been forgotten about. The floorboard creaked again. In her head she repeated, *Please, please, please, please. Please say they didn't see me.*

With steady footsteps the teachers continued down the corridor. Minutes passed in complete silence. It was so dark she couldn't see a thing. Alex felt around cautiously, hoping to avoid the spiky creatures. She was in a very small room; she could tell that much. Crawling forwards, her hands touched what she thought was the door. That moment, something brushed her face and she jumped. *A spider's web?* she thought in alarm. Alex swiped the air to bat away whatever it was and realised it was in fact a thin rope or cord. *For a light, perhaps*, she thought hopefully. When she was completely sure that nobody was outside the cupboard, Alex pulled it.

A light above flickered weakly, as if waking up after a long sleep, filling the room with a faint yellow glow. Alex saw then that the hedgehogs she'd fallen on weren't hedgehogs at all. She was sitting amongst a huge pile of old brooms.

Bottles of cleaning fluid and buckets sat on shelves covered in dust. On the door hung moth-eaten aprons which couldn't have been worn for years. Alex had stumbled into an old, forgotten broom cupboard. It was possible, judging by the state of the place, that nobody at the Time Academy even remembered the cupboard existed.

Alex settled into a space between a mop and a feather duster. She closed her eyes and tuned her ears to the silence. She could quite happily stay in this cupboard for ever, she thought. She was safe here amongst the brooms. The world outside, with its scary new technology and unanswered questions, was far away. In the cupboard, everything was exactly as it seemed. A mop was just an old mop. A broom was just a broom.

For the first time in Alex's life, she was facing a problem that she didn't know how to solve. She'd always thought that, at least with Uncle Henry's help, there was no problem she couldn't work out. Even when confronted by an impossibly hard maths puzzle, the right answer would eventually appear, as if it had been staring her in the face all the time. Now, she had no idea what the right thing to do was. She couldn't see how everything could possibly work out OK. And nobody was here to help her or save the day. Her fate rested entirely in her own two hands.

Alex stared hopelessly at the back of the cupboard

door, thinking about nothing except for how sorry she was for herself. She imagined growing old in the cupboard. Being found, eventually, years from now, an elderly woman with grey hair and no teeth, who'd made friends with the brooms and mops, and given them all names. That was her fate, she decided, so she'd better get used to the idea.

But as she slumped down, nestling her head on a broom pillow and pulling an old rug over her as a blanket, she had a sudden image of Uncle Henry tucking her in, as he did every night. *What would happen to Uncle Henry if she didn't return?* He would be worried sick if she vanished with no trace. And besides that, who would be there to make sure he ate more than pickled eggs for dinner and opened the curtains once in a while, and stopped playing video games when his eyes started to cross? He needed Alex as much as she needed him.

She was feeling desperately sad when, for a split second, the lightbulb above her head flickered brightly. It was only a moment, but it was enough for her to see it – a glint of bronze against the dark wood of the door. She crawled closer on her hands and knees. With her finger she traced its cold surface. It was a notice – or maybe a plaque. The metal was dull and covered with dark spots, with only a faint trace of writing still visible. Alex wiped hard at the letters with the bottom of her shirt, until she could make out the words. She read them to herself in a whisper.

IN THIS BROOM CUPBOARD, EMILY
WILDING DAVISON HID HERSELF,
ILLEGALLY, DURING THE NIGHT
OF THE 1911 CENSUS.
SHE WAS A BRAVE SUFFRAGETTE
CAMPAIGNING FOR VOTES FOR
WOMEN AT A TIME WHEN PARLIAMENT
DENIED THEM THAT RIGHT.

Alex read it again. She'd learned about the suffragettes at school and so knew that they had fought to give women the right to vote. This broom cupboard was part of history. Gerty would gladly add it to her collection, given half the chance. The last person to hide within its walls had done so because she'd wanted to change the world. Alex was hiding in the cupboard because she was too afraid to leave. This realisation made her feel deeply ashamed.

'If Emily Wilding Davison can be brave, so can I,' Alex said, getting to her feet. 'I've got to at least try.'

At that moment, the bell in the clock tower thundered. *DONG . . . DONG . . . DONG . . . DONG . . .* As the last chime struck, a distant tremble of voices and movement began. The floorboards beneath her feet started vibrating. Alex pressed her ear close to the door. Students, lots of them by the sound of it, were marching down the corridor. This was her chance.

Gently, Alex turned the handle of the cupboard door. She remained still as the crowd of students got nearer, and louder, until she could tell they were right outside. Then, when it sounded like they were about to pass by, she gently pushed the door open and slipped out.

Alex had been right to think there were a lot of them. There must have been several year groups, all walking together in a snaking line of green. None of them noticed her leave the cupboard; they were too busy chatting excitedly about something. She was relieved to see Meera's plait ahead in the line. She was talking to a boy with floppy hair.

'I want to get a good seat,' he said, trying to cut ahead of his classmates. 'One at the front so I can see everything.'

Meera looked thoroughly unimpressed. 'Well, I definitely don't,' she said. 'I hate that they're making us all go. I feel really sorry for him. Imagine being kicked out of the Academy. My parents would kill me.'

Alex's belly jumped with a mixture of excitement and fear. *They must be talking about Jasper,* she thought. 'Meera!' she called, catching up. 'Meera, wait!'

'It's you!' Meera was shocked. 'I didn't think I'd be seeing you again after the stunt you pulled at lunch earlier. Thought you'd be in Disciplinary for a week!'

'I guess I was lucky,' Alex said, not untruthfully. 'Where are we going?'

The boy with floppy hair looked at her as if she was very stupid. 'To the tribunal. They're deciding what to do with Jasper Song.'

Alex's heart plummeted. She was too late! Gerty had been clear that she had to find Jasper *before* his sentencing, and she had failed. Even so, through her despair, Alex felt a thrill knowing she would soon see Jasper again. Part of her thought that as soon as they were back together everything would be better – they could figure out a way to escape.

They followed the line of students through the hall and into an enormous rectangular room. Stretched across either side of the room facing each other were rows of wooden benches covered with green leather cushions. Some benches near the front were already occupied by older students talking seriously to one another in low voices. Near the entrance, a teacher was directing students to their seats like an usher at the theatre.

'You there. Don't stop in the middle of the bench,' he said with a sigh. 'Move all the way along. That's it, keep going!'

Alex and Meera were waved towards a bench in the second to back row. From this vantage point, Alex surveyed the room. Hanging at one end of the room was an enormous sheet of green velvet. Stitched in gold across the fabric was a list of rules. Meera caught Alex staring at it.

'Those are the ten sacred Laws of Time,' she explained. 'I think Jasper broke about half of them in one go.'

Alex quickly scanned the list.

THE INTERNATIONAL LAWS OF TIME

1. **Time Travellers are strictly forbidden from changing the course of history during their visit to the past. This includes both inadvertent and deliberate actions.**

2. **Time Travellers are strictly forbidden from revealing the existence of Time Travel, or their identity as a Time Traveller, to any person from the past.**

3. Time Travellers are strictly forbidden from revealing information about the future, or information originating from the future, to any person from the past.

4. Time Travellers are strictly forbidden from speaking to or otherwise engaging with any person from the past, except where it is unavoidable or necessary to prevent the exposure of Time Travel.

5. Time Travellers are strictly forbidden from making, or attempting to make, unregulated Time Travel trips. All Time Travel must be approved and regulated by the Time Minister.

6. Time Travellers are strictly forbidden from taking any items from the past.

7. Time Travellers are strictly forbidden from visiting, or attempting to visit, the future. They are only permitted to do so as part of their return journey after visiting the past, as regulated by the Time Minister.

8. Time Travellers must carry Time Passports at all times. Time Passports must be renewed on an annual basis, at the discretion of the Time Minister.

9. The use of Time Crystals is regulated and restricted by the Time Minister. Only those with special permission from the Time Minister may create, own, handle or use a Time Crystal.

10. Time Travellers must follow the guidance of their supervisory Time Guard throughout the duration of

their visit to the past. Time Guards have the power to caution and arrest those under suspicion of breaking Time Law, according to the Time Guard code of conduct.

Positioned in front of the velvet fabric was a grand chair rather like a throne. Its back was several metres high with a carved wooden canopy hanging over the top. Above it hung a small white clock.

'Who sits there?' Alex whispered, and Meera smiled patiently.

'That's where the Time Minister usually sits. Or sometimes, Ms Crale. I don't think she's meant to, not really. But I bet she does today.'

'What about Jasper? Where is he?'

'They won't bring him in until everyone's sat down. He'll stand over there, in front of the whole school, all the teachers and the senior Time Guards.' Meera pointed to the aisle that ran down the centre of the benches. 'You'll know who they are because they wear a special Time Guard uniform. They'll hear what he has to say and after that the Time Minister will decide what to do with him. He'll be thrown out of the Time Academy for sure, though. Some people have been saying they'll even strip him of his Time Passport, if you can imagine that.'

'What happens then?'

The girl looked puzzled, before continuing. 'Well, obviously that would be the end of his career as a Time Guard. But not just that. Without his Time Passport he wouldn't be able to travel through time *ever again*. Not even on holiday. He'd be stuck.'

Alex was sure she would cry. If they took away Jasper's Time Passport, she would certainly never see him again. She blinked away the tears. Now wasn't the time to draw attention to herself.

It wasn't long before all the benches were full. What with the green benches, the green carpets and the green uniforms, Alex had never seen so much green in one room. The low buzz of chatter became louder as the room filled. It seemed that even for Time Academy students the temptation to chat about something as juicy as the tribunal was too much to resist.

Then, in an instant, as if the air in the room had been sucked out, the room was plunged into silence. If a feather had fallen, you would have heard it hit the floor. Making her way across the carpet was a tall woman with hair the colour of squid ink. Alex recognised her at once. Her face, just as it had been in the alleyway in Murford when Alex last saw her, was fierce, sharp-angled. She positioned herself in the centre of the room and waited while a line of teachers in green robes walked to the front benches and took their seats. Alex noticed that there was no sign of Mr Parrot.

'Is that Ms Crale, in the gold dress?' she whispered to Meera, who gave a quick nod. So that explains it, Alex thought. The woman who had come to take Jasper that day in the alleyway was the head teacher of the Time Academy. She looked as impatient and stern as she had before, only now Alex understood how powerful she was. Moments later, a line of important-looking adults walked into the room. They were wearing green suits similar to those the students wore, except with bright gold embroidery along the arms, lapels and buttonholes. She knew from what Meera had said that they were senior Time Guards.

When they were all seated, Ms Crale began.

'This is a dark day in the history of our great school,' she said, calmly. 'The Time Academy was set up many years ago with one purpose in mind. To protect and defend our most precious gift: Time. It is our sacred duty – every single one of us – to ensure that the river of Time is allowed to run its course. It is our duty to ensure that all our fellow travellers through Time return safely to their beginnings and, eventually, as we all do, reach their ends. We are defenders of Time, the oldest form of justice in the universe.'

She paused and there was complete silence in the room. 'Needless to say, anyone who betrays the sacred Laws of Time puts everyone at risk. They threaten our past, our present and our future. There is no crime more dangerous than that.'

Alex was pressed forwards in her seat, listening intently to every horrible word. She wanted to shout out, to tell the head teacher that Jasper hadn't meant to break Time Law. That he wasn't dangerous or a threat. It was all a misunderstanding. *Wait for Jasper*, she told herself, chewing her lip to keep the words from escaping out her mouth.

'The Time Minister will make the final judgment,' continued Ms Crale, 'but I ask you all to consider seriously the testimony of the young man who will come before us shortly. Listen closely. Suspend your judgement until you have heard the facts. And reflect, as you make your decision, on the duty that unites us all as Time Guards.'

The woman took a seat on the throne-like chair. As she did, the rest of the room let out their breath collectively. A few people shuffled in their seats.

Meera put her hand to her mouth and leaned towards Alex's ear.

'Told you she'd sit there,' she whispered. 'She's definitely after the Time Minister's job.'

'Why do you think that?' Alex whispered back.

'She's been head teacher for decades. And the Time Minister is so old now that I suppose Ms Crale feels it's about time someone else took over.'

Alex opened her mouth to ask another question. But before she could speak, the door creaked open. Into the room, accompanied by a stern-looking man wearing the Time Guard uniform, walked a boy. His black hair stuck up on his head like flames. He was staring resolutely down at his boots, a look of determined anguish on his face.

Without a second's thought, Alex was on her feet. She clutched the back of the bench in front of her. 'Jasper!' she shouted, before she could stop herself. Her voice bounced around the four walls.

Suddenly, every single pair of eyes in the room was turned right towards her, including the eyes of the boy who she had come all this way to find. Whispers spread like fire, surrounding her in all directions. For a moment she didn't care. Alex had finally done what she came all this way to do. She had found Jasper.

But then she saw the look on his face. In her imagination, when she'd thought about this moment, Jasper was as pleased to see her as she was him. Looking down at him now, though, even from a distance, she could see he was anything but pleased.

In fact, Jasper looked terrified.

CHAPTER SIXTEEN

Just in the Nick of Time

Ms Crale had risen from her seat. At the sight of Alex, she made a noise that sounded like a strangled bird. She gazed in utter disbelief at Alex, then at Jasper, and back to Alex. And then, she bowed.

'Your Excellency, is it really you? Here?' she gasped. 'But that's not possible.'

Alex craned her neck to try and see who had entered the room, but the students in the rows in front of her were now standing and her view was blocked.

Slowly at first, and then very quickly, a buzz spread across the hall.

'Look, it's really her!' Alex heard somebody say.

'No way, it can't be,' said another.

'That's impossible!'

'But it has to be!'

'She came for him!'

Everyone was distracted by whoever had come in the room. Perhaps it was the Time Minister, Alex thought. And then she realised that now was her chance to get to the front and to Jasper.

'Excuse me, excuse me,' Alex squeezed down the bench, apologising to an open-mouthed Meera as she passed her. To her surprise, every person she encountered sprung out of her way with a look of alarm. Some even gave her a small bow as she passed.

'Don't let her go,' commanded Ms Crale. 'By the Order of Time, stop that girl!'

Nobody was paying Ms Crale the slightest bit of attention. Even the boy with the floppy hair jumped out of Alex's way with a look of utter horror on his face. Alex came out at the end of her row and ran down the aisle between the benches. And then Jasper, who had been frozen to the spot, expressionless, burst into the widest smile possible.

Alex ran at Jasper which such force she almost knocked him out of his boots. She hugged him tightly for what seemed like an hour before letting go.

'I didn't think I would see you ever again.'

'You weren't supposed to!' Jasper said, looking at her like he couldn't quite believe she was here.

Alex was so overcome with happiness at being reunited with her friend that she'd almost forgotten the difficult situation they now found themselves in. But, in the periphery of her vision, the image of Ms Crale now came to her attention.

'Apprehend her,' Ms Crale said, staring coldly at the guard who'd accompanied Jasper into the room. 'And the boy.'

The guard hesitated. 'But I can't, madam. Not if the girl is who I think she is. And she is who I think she is, isn't she?'

Alex's stomach churned with anticipation. *Who exactly does he think I am?*

'Of course she is. But that doesn't matter,' Ms Crale snapped. 'Do what *I* say.'

The guard straightened up, chin high in the air. 'That's impossible. My oath as a Time Guard is to protect the past, present and future. She is all three of those things. I will not break it for anything.'

'Don't be ridiculous, I am the head teacher of this school. You follow my orders.'

'I follow *her* orders, actually.'

The guard turned his back to Ms Crale. Solemnly, he made a low bow in Alex's direction.

'Come on, let's go,' Jasper said to Alex, pulling at

her hand. But Alex hesitated. What did the guard mean, saying that he followed *her* orders? How could she be the past, present and future?

'Alex, let's go!'

Jasper had already walked halfway down the aisle and was waiting for her to join him. This is what she'd come to do: to break out Jasper. Besides, she could hear Ms Crale calling angrily for more Time Guards to apprehend her and she knew their time was running out.

'Thank you for your help,' she said to the guard, who visibly blushed. She looked for Meera in the crowd and gave her a smile and wave goodbye. Then she turned on her heel and ran towards the door.

They sprinted through the lobby, down a corridor and into the octagonal hall.

'It's this way!' Jasper tugged her towards the door on the right. 'But what's the plan once we get outside? They'll come looking for us. That guard was nice, but most of them are too scared to stand up to Ms Crale.'

'Gerty is waiting at the entrance.' *Or I hope she still is,* thought Alex. She'd been in the Time Academy much longer than she'd planned. There was a chance Gerty would have got tired of waiting and left.

'Who?'

'A friend, you'll see. Come on.'

They hurtled towards the wooden door and down the steps into the corridor with the paintings and stone statues. They were halfway down the corridor when they came to a screeching halt. It seemed, at least at first, that one of the statues had jumped out at them. But then Alex realised it wasn't a statue at all.

'Well, well, well,' Mr Parrot sneered. 'So, *this* is what you were up to. Breaking out our little criminal.'

'Mr Parrot,' said Jasper, softly, 'you don't understand.'

'I understand perfectly. I understand that this girl is trying to help you escape. And that the Time Minister will be none too pleased to hear about it. Think of the reward I will be given for stopping you. I'll be promoted straight out of that blasted library.'

'No,' said Jasper, firmly. 'The opposite is true, in fact. If you don't let us go, you'll be in more trouble with the Time Minister than you can imagine.'

'What do you know, child, about the Time Minister? You're only a Time Guard in training. One who is about to lose his Time Licence for good.'

'I can't tell you. You just have to believe me.'

'I do, do I?' Mr Parrot said, scornfully.

'Telling you would break Time Law.'

'I didn't think Time Law had much currency with you.' He grabbed both Jasper and Alex by their waistcoats. 'I'm bored with this now. I've spent half the afternoon locked in the library thanks to your accomplice there. You're both coming with me straight to Ms Crale.'

He started dragging them both backwards. Jasper leaned towards Mr Parrot and whispered something in his ear. He released his grip from their waistcoats in an instant.

'She's who?' he roared. He looked wildly at Alex. 'But . . . but . . . she can't be. How?'

Alex stared at Jasper. What had he told Mr Parrot? And why would he share the secret with *him* but not tell her? She had come all this way to save Jasper and he was still hiding the truth from her. A niggling worry that had been growing deep in her stomach nudged its way into her brain. *Maybe I become someone terrible* she thought, *maybe I do something so awful Jasper doesn't want me to know. Maybe all this time he was supposed to be protecting* other people *from me. Maybe that's why everyone here seems scared of me.*

Mr Parrot dropped to his knees. 'Forgive me,' he breathed. 'Forgive me. I didn't know.'

'Um, sure,' Alex said, bewildered. She looked

curiously at Jasper, who shrugged. 'But only if you let us go. And – and promise you'll start being nicer to people.'

'Whatever you say, your Excellency.' He shuffled towards Alex's boots and tried to kiss them. She recoiled, horrified.

'Euugh! Stop that!'

Jasper laughed so hard his hair shook. 'Come on, Alex. Before he starts offering to peel you grapes.'

They left the man mumbling, 'I didn't know, I didn't know, believe me I didn't know!' to himself. Bursting through the doors and emerging at the top of the steps, Alex scanned the hall and breathed a huge sigh of relief. Gerty was exactly where Alex had left her hours before, pacing back and forth. Gerty danced on the spot when she saw them flying down the stairs towards her.

'I found him, Gerty!'

'I can see that well enough, kiddo. But no time to gloat. Let's get out of here!'

The three of them crossed the stone floor, past the unicorn and lion and then they were out into the warm afternoon air. They found their Cy-cle where they'd left it. Alex and Gerty climbed on the saddle and somehow, after lots of effort, Jasper managed to fit in the basket at the front of the bike.

'Jasper, put this on.' Gerty handed him a shabby-looking helmet. 'Make sure it's nice and tight.'

There wasn't time for Alex to ask where *her* helmet was. Ms Crale could burst out the doors at any moment. Slightly wobbly now, with three on a bike made for one, they set off.

CHAPTER SEVENTEEN

The Return

'I won't lie, kiddo, I didn't expect to see you again.'

Gerty pulled up the Cy-cle beside the boarded windows of Wandle & Swish. With some difficulty, Jasper climbed out of the basket. They hadn't been followed, as far as Alex could tell. She'd kept looking behind them throughout the journey to make sure. Once, she'd almost lost her balance and fallen right off the bike, after which Gerty shouted at her to keep eyes front.

'Where are we?' asked Jasper.

'This is where Gerty keeps her collection.'

'What kind of collection?'

'We've got some questions for you too, boy-o,' said Gerty. 'Don't take that helmet off until we get inside.' Jasper shared a worried look with Alex. Gerty pushed open the doors and Jasper and Alex stepped inside behind her.

They followed Gerty quickly up the stairs. Alex whispered to Jasper, 'You're going to love it up here. It's full of wonderful things. Quite a few old books too.'

When they reached the top of the stairs, Jasper was just as excited as Alex had thought he'd be. As excited as she had been the day before. Alex followed him down a row of musical instruments – cellos, harps, DJ turntables, bagpipes and many others that she couldn't name. Resting against a cabinet was an instrument almost as tall as Alex made of shiny dark wood. According to the label, it was a sitar which had once belonged to the musician Ravi Shankar. Jasper gently touched the carved wood and brushed the strings, enjoying the sound they made. A little further on sat a harpsichord which had been built for the Empress of Russia, Catherine the Great. It looked to Alex like a strangely shaped but beautiful piano, its lid propped open and keys ready to be played. Further on still were rows of electric guitars belonging to rock stars throughout history, drums of various sizes, a line-up of microphones and glittering stage outfits. Jasper spent some time strumming tunelessly at one of the guitars (taken from a young Jimi Hendrix) before allowing himself to be dragged by Alex to the next aisle.

Here they found endless shelves of toys: giant glass jars of marbles; piles of yo-yos, some made of wood, some made of clay, and some made of brightly coloured plastic; china dolls lined up on shelves beside rag dolls and hundreds of shiny stone animal figurines. Bright red toy cars sat next to tiny bronze chariots and mouse-sized wooden horses with wheels instead of feet. A network of train sets whizzed around tracks; a full cavalry of rocking horses stood waiting for their riders; miniature plastic dinosaurs were locked in fierce battles.

'Gerty, you're a Time Trader!' Jasper was breathless and wide-eyed. 'We learned about people like you at the Academy in our Time Crime lessons.'

Gerty laughed. 'I'm sure we didn't come across too favourably.'

'Well, no,' admitted Jasper. 'The Time Guards aren't very fond of you.'

'That, son, is what we call an understatement. They lock people up for smuggling so much as a toothbrush through time. If they saw all this,' Gerty waved her arms around, 'I can only imagine what they'd do.'

Jasper frowned. 'I think I've heard them speaking

about you before. They don't know who you are, just that there's a thief with a big collection – although I doubt they know *how* big. There's a reward for your capture.'

'My reputation precedes me,' Gerty said, happily. 'I used to teach at the Academy, you know – and I enjoy giving my former colleagues the old run around.' She sighed. 'One thing's for sure, though – after today's events they will be doubling up security at the station.'

Alex swallowed anxiously. The coaches were the only way she knew of to get back to Murford.

It seemed Jasper might have had the same worry, as his face looked tense. 'The Time Guards will be tracking me already. We shouldn't stay in one place for too long.'

'We're safe here, don't worry,' said Gerty. 'I've made special arrangements that stop anyone detecting our chips. So long as you're within these walls, you're safe.'

Jasper still looked worried and Alex understood why. 'They'll be able to track us right to your doorstep, though,' she said.

Gerty gave them a reassuring smile. 'That's why I told him to wear that helmet. You can take it off now, by the way.'

Jasper looked puzzled for a moment. He unbuckled

the helmet and looked at it. A few seconds later, a knowing smile spread across his face.

'It blocks out the signal!'

'Bingo.'

He returned the helmet to Gerty and she slipped it into one of the huge pockets in her gown.

'Now that's all settled, Jasper. I think it's time we heard your side of the story,' she said firmly. 'This young lady has travelled a long way to hear it. Mind you, be careful not to reveal *too* much. There are some secrets about the future which Alex simply can't be told. It would be too risky. It could change the course of history. But you must tell her everything you can. It's the least she deserves.'

Jasper sat side-saddle on one of the rocking horses. He had the weary look of someone who had been keeping a secret for a long time. Alex smiled encouragingly at him, trying her best to contain her anticipation even though she could hear her heartbeat through her ribcage. Finally, she was going to get some answers. In that moment, she felt like Mr Parrot, such was her eagerness to read Jasper's mind.

'The thing is,' Jasper began. 'I never really wanted to go to the Time Academy. I didn't even apply. Most people's parents take care of that for them, but my parents passed away when I was a baby. I grew up in foster care. So, when I was selected, nobody could believe it. I thought it was a joke or something. I told Ms Crale that, but she insisted it wasn't a mistake. It's an incredible honour for most people to be chosen. But I knew from the moment I started that it wasn't the place for me.'

'It was about halfway through my first year at the Time Academy when Ms Crale called me to her office. She said she had a special assignment for me, that I had been requested for the job directly by the Time Minister. I didn't understand why they'd want *me*. My grades are low in almost every single subject. I was bottom of the class in World History. I got twenty-one per cent in my last Physics of Time exam. Don't even get me started on Cyber Surveillance. The only subject I was any good at was Language Through Time. But still Ms Crale said I was the boy for the job. She didn't look too happy about it, but she kept saying that she was following orders. So, they sent me to Murford. My job was to watch over you, Alex, to make sure that you didn't come to any harm.'

'But why me?' Alex interrupted.

Gerty cleared her throat. 'Let the boy finish.'

'I was meant to keep my distance from you, to blend

in like they teach us at the Academy. Sit in the back of your classes and pretend like you didn't exist. But I messed it all up.'

'How?' asked Alex, and Gerty shot her a look.

'The day before I was supposed to start at your school, I was doing some research, watching you and Uncle Henry preparing for the party. I saw all the food and decorations you'd made. And I felt so sad when nobody turned up. I guess I knew what it was like not to have many friends. I left for home but halfway there I turned around again. I couldn't help myself. I ran back to your house and rang your doorbell.'

Gerty looked aghast. 'Are you not familiar with Time Law? We're not allowed to intervene, no matter what happens.'

'I know,' Jasper said, miserably. 'Like I said, I messed everything up.'

'What happened next?' asked Alex.

'Well, we became friends.' Jasper smiled at her, but the smile quickly faded. 'I tried to hide what was happening from the Academy, but eventually word got back to my teachers. I was ordered to come back straight away. I wanted to talk to you first, Alex. To tell you everything right there in the alleyway. But Ms Crale arrived before I could. Since then, I've been in

Disciplinary waiting for the tribunal. I never expected to see you at the Time Academy. I thought I was seeing things at first when you shouted my name.'

Alex remembered the look on Jasper's face when he'd seen her at the tribunal. 'I was worried you were angry with me.'

'Angry? I was shocked. And a bit afraid. No one has ever travelled *forwards* from their own time before.'

'You were happy to see me?' Alex felt unaccountably nervous waiting for the answer.

'Yes! You're my best friend. Hanging out with you and Uncle Henry made me feel like I finally fit in somewhere.'

Alex beamed. Their conversation was interrupted by a deep sob. They looked around to see Gerty dabbing at her eyes. 'What a pair of rule-breakers you are. Between the two of you, you've smashed all the Time Laws ever invented.' She sobbed again. 'It makes me so proud.'

Jasper and Alex both looked at each other. He was the first to break the silence. 'So, now you know everything.'

'No, I don't!' Alex spluttered. 'Not *everything*. I don't know why you came to Murford. Why you were told to watch after *me*. Who do I become in the future? You can tell me now. Please!'

She was starting to get annoyed. She deserved to know this secret – which, after all, was about *her* life, *her* future. She had a right to know more than anybody else.

Jasper opened and closed his mouth. He was about to speak, when a strange whirring sound cut him off. The three of them look around for the source of the noise. It was Gerty who realised first.

'Arthur Foxtail.' She gasped. 'What are you doing here?'

Arthur was leaning against one of the toy shelves, throwing a yo-yo down and up, down and up. This time he wasn't wearing a tunic or fake brown teeth. He wore a pair of jeans, a sleeveless denim jacket and a white T-shirt. There was a smirk on his lips and a slightly unsettling look in his eyes, which were locked on Alex.

'Go on, don't be rude,' he said. 'Answer the girl, Jasper. Or, if you won't, shall I?'

CHAPTER EIGHTEEN

Dinner with a Difference

'I don't know why it took me so long to realise.' Arthur spun the yo-yo around his wrist. 'I should have known straight away, that day at the station. We've met, you and I, more times than you know. I was there when you were born. Your first day at school. Your last day at school, come to think of it, but I guess you haven't got that far yet. But I never expected to see you here. Took my brain a while to catch up with itself.'

Jasper was the first to reply. 'Who are you?' he asked, taken aback at the sudden interruption.

'Good evening, Arthur,' Gerty cut in, looking a bit surprised herself. 'Don't be alarmed, Jasper. He's an associate of mine in the Time Trading business. I hope you're not here to make a nuisance of yourself, Arthur.'

Arthur didn't take his eyes away from Alex. 'I took

some algebra homework from you once. It's here somewhere, if you look hard enough.'

'What are you talking about?' said Alex, crossly. 'We've never met, until yesterday.'

'You've no idea who you are, do you? Who you'll *become*, I should say.'

'No, I don't have any idea,' said Alex, 'because nobody will tell me. I'm starting to think you're all wrong about this. I'm not anybody special. I'm a nobody.'

'Alex Nobody,' Arthur said softly. 'Is that who you think you are?'

Alex's mouth dropped open like a cod. She had a vision of the careers lesson where Mrs Wright had called her exactly that, much to the amusement of her peers. It seemed like it had happened in a different world now. But surely Arthur couldn't know about that.

'Please,' she said. 'Is it terrible? Am I famous for doing something bad? Is that why you won't tell me?'

'Arthur,' said Gerty sharply, before he could say a word in reply. 'You know you can't give this girl the answers she wants. It would break Time Law. Now, normally I don't worry too much about breaking Time Law but this is where I draw the line. Telling her who she becomes could change the future. It might stop

Alex becoming the person she is destined to become. I don't know who that is and frankly I don't care to find out. The kid is fine by me whoever she becomes. So, what are you trying to achieve here? I don't believe you're going to hand the girl in to the authorities. It's not your style.'

Arthur looked disgusted. 'Hand her in? I'd never do anything to help those cheese-brains at the Time Academy. Obviously, I'm not going to hand the kid in.'

Gerty's eyes narrowed in suspicion. 'What are you after then? More money, is that it?'

Arthur made an offended face. 'You think so little of me, Gert, after all this time working together. When we've always been as thick as . . . well, as thieves. It hurts, it really does. I was simply curious. Thought you might have engineered all of this, Gerty – pulled off the most daring smuggling operation in the history of Time Trading. Smuggled an actual person from the past. Wanted to get a slice of the action, if I could. And then, when I realised who the girl was, I couldn't believe it.' He nodded at Alex. 'Must have been your hair that threw me off – you don't look yourself without your normal style. And who in their right mind would have expected to bump into someone like *you* in the coach station? It should have been impossible. So you can't blame me for taking so long to figure it all out. It had been bugging me all day. Why did I know your face? And then this afternoon it came to me. As soon as I realised who you are, I knew had to find out more. Then I heard this young lad's story just now. And what can I say, it warms my heart.'

'I wasn't under the impression you had much of a heart, Arthur,' said Gerty. 'All you care about is thieving and general skulduggery.'

'I have a heart of gold.' He grinned. 'And a heart for gold.'

'Well now that you understand,' Gerty said, still eyeing him warily, 'you can help me get her back to her own time. How's that for a slice of the action? You'll be paid for your assistance, of course.'

'What? I'm not going back yet!' Alex was horrified at the thought. 'I'm not leaving without finding out what this secret is. And I'm certainly not leaving Jasper here like this. It's all my fault he's in trouble in the first place.'

'You have to leave, kiddo.' Gerty looked at her sadly. 'You can't stay in the wrong time. It isn't right. And you won't become the person you're destined to become if you're stuck in the future. You need to follow your own path, in your own time.'

'But if I go what will happen to you, Jasper?'

'Don't worry about me,' he replied, running a hand through his dark hair. 'I'll be fine. Think of Uncle Henry. You've got to get back to him, remember?'

Alex's eyes widened. Jasper was right. What about her uncle? How could she forget him? 'Could I come back here? Sneak on another coach, like I did this time.'

'It won't be that simple,' Gerty cut in. 'The Time Guards will be extra vigilant now.'

Alex swallowed. 'Jasper, are you saying that I can't see you ever again?'

They were all silent. Jasper looked like he might cry.

'I'm sorry, kiddo. You're going back first thing tomorrow morning. There's no two ways about it. If you hand yourself in to the Time Guards at the coach station and tell them who you are, they will escort you back to your own time where you belong. The three of us will have to stay well clear, of course, to make sure we aren't apprehended. But they'll have no choice but to take you back home – they can't arrest somebody from the past. I know you don't like to leave Jasper, but that's what has to happen.'

'But—'

'First coach tomorrow morning.' Gerty's voice was

stern. She placed a sympathetic hand on Alex's shoulder and left it there for several seconds. Then continued brightly, 'Right, we'll be needing some dinner soon. Arthur, come give me a hand in the kitchen will you.'

'Coming, matron.' Arthur gave a smile which showed every one of his brilliantly white teeth. He skipped behind Gerty down a passageway leading to the kitchen area. When they were gone, Alex looked at Jasper seriously.

'Listen,' she whispered, 'Gerty won't help us, but there has to be some way we can fix this. We'll find a way to stop you going to prison. Or we could sneak you back to Murford with me. If we put our heads together and think really hard, we'll work it out. That's what Uncle Henry and I do whenever we encounter a problem.'

Jasper looked miserably down at his boots. 'We can't. You've got to go back tomorrow.'

'But . . . but . . .' replied Alex, taken aback. She had been expecting him to say anything but that. 'You're my friend, Jasper. My best friend.'

'You're mine too.'

'Well, that means something important.' Alex flushed. 'It means we must find a way to stay together even if it seems impossible. Before you, my best friend was a computer,' she added with a small smile. 'I don't really want to go back to that.'

'Thanks, I think.' He laughed, though his eyes were still filled with sadness. 'And thanks for coming all this way to find me. Breaking International Time Law and all that.'

'You broke it first.' She smiled. 'Uncle Henry won't believe it when I tell him about all of this.'

'I think you could be right about that.'

'If I go back home, what will happen to you?'

'I could stay here in Gerty's collection for ever, if she'll have me, and be safe. Or go on the run, try to keep one step ahead of the Time Guards and Ms Crale for the rest of my life. She seemed pretty determined to lock me up for good and she usually gets her way. But I'll stay out of prison for as long as I can.'

'They'll find you eventually, they're bound too. And then you'll go to jail! And lose your Time Passport.'

'That wouldn't be so bad. I've always preferred reading about the past to visiting it. As long as I have a book I can do all the Time Travel I like. Without any of the danger.'

'But—'

That moment, Arthur announced his return with a loud sneeze. 'Awfully sorry to interrupt. The dust in here does terrible things to my nose.' He sneezed violently again three times. 'We need your help setting the table. Gerty can't remember where she keeps the cutlery. Seems to think it could be with the Egyptian mummies. I keep telling her she needs a better storage system.'

Alex and Jasper followed Arthur in a thoughtful silence towards dinner. They emerged in a space with a large table and four stools at the centre. Glasses and plates were laid out haphazardly, along with napkins and a jug of water. Gerty appeared pushing a trolley with an assortment of dishes, pots and tins. A cocktail of smells filled the air, not all of them entirely appetising. Arthur left in search of cutlery while Alex and Jasper helped to transfer the dishes to the table. On closer inspection, they saw it wasn't a dining table at all. The surface was lined with green felt and there were holes in each corner.

'It belonged to the writer Mark Twain,' Gerty explained. 'He loved billiards, and food for that matter, so I thought it would make a fitting dining table.'

'It's perfect,' said Jasper, enthusiastically.

Arthur returned with two fistfuls of cutlery which included chopsticks, bronze spoons, a few seashells, a two-pronged, very pointy fork, and several plastic knives. From the bunch Alex picked a neon pink spork that seemed like the safest option.

Once they were all seated, Gerty poured grape juice into each of their glasses. She cleared her throat theatrically. 'Before we eat, there is something I would like to say.'

Arthur sighed impatiently, but Gerty ignored him. Her eyebrows bristled importantly, making her look more like an owl than ever. 'In my life, I've travelled through history and met many people from different places and walks of life. But everyone I've met has had something in common. They all came together over a good meal. It's something that bonds us, I think, as human beings. It's not only about filling our bellies – though it's a lot about that I admit. It's about something more, something special. I hope the meal we are about to eat will give us all some comfort tonight, as we prepare to say goodbye tomorrow.'

She launched her glass high in the air, and the others did the same. 'To friendship. And the bonds that bring us together.'

They sipped their juice and Arthur shouted, 'Hear hear!' Alex remained silent. Not because she didn't want to drink to friendship. But because she had no intention at all of saying goodbye.

'Now can we start?' Arthur said, hungrily. But Gerty had beaten him to it and was already heaping green beans on to her plate.

'Pass me the honey, please.' Gerty pointed at a ceramic pot. 'From bees belonging to Julius Caesar, do you remember, Arth?'

'Oh, yes,' he replied, wincing, 'I can still feel the stings.'

Alex suddenly had a horrible suspicion that *all* the food on the table was from the past. The thought of eating food hundreds of years older than she was made her queasy.

'It looks lovely. Is it all . . . safe to eat?' she asked.

Gerty sniffed. 'Yes, of course it is. Arthur brings back food from his travels when he can. But only things that will keep.'

Still unsure, but not wanting to offend Gerty further, Alex picked up a glass jar and spooned out some of the contents on to her plate. It looked like piccalilli, or perhaps a kind of chutney.

'Why, that's Jane Austen's famous home-made preserve,' Gerty said.

From another jar, Alex took some pickled gherkins, and a few carrots from a tin can.

'And those,' said Gerty with relish, 'were taken on a

famous expedition to the Arctic in 1845. All the men on the ship died and some historians suspected it was because of the canned food they ate – but that's nonsense. These carrots are perfectly safe and delicious. People worry too much.'

Alex and Jasper looked at each other, then quietly both pushed the carrots to the side of their plates.

'You'll be needing your strength for the journey. This was good enough for the Vikings on long trips across the sea, so it will be good enough for you.' Gerty handed Alex a dish which seemed to contain strips of dried fish. Alex passed it quickly on to Arthur.

'You might prefer these.' He handed her a saucepan with a wink. She looked inside and gasped. It was her favourite food – baked beans, like she cooked with her uncle. It made her wonder rather uneasily how Arthur knew she liked baked beans. But on the other hand, she was ravenous and gulped down the lot in minutes.

After the beans, Alex ate some noodle soup, the instant kind from a packet, and some rubbery hotdog sausages. Then she sat back, feeling very full.

'That was a feast,' Jasper said around his last mouthful of tinned mashed potato. Mrs Puff, standing on the table, her entire head in the baked beans saucepan, meowed in agreement.

Arthur picked bits of dried fish from his teeth with his fingernails. Jasper hid a yawn with his hand. The food had brought a sudden wave of sleepiness over them all.

'An early night is on the cards, my dears,' said Gerty, clapping her hands together. 'You'll need a good night's sleep ahead of tomorrow's journey home.'

Alex nodded. *I'm not going anywhere*, she was thinking. Not without Jasper. 'Are you sure they'll take me back? They won't arrest me too?'

'No, they won't. The Time Guards will take great care to return you to where you came from. All you need to do is introduce yourself and they'll take care of the rest.'

'Would they take me back to the same time I left?' She was thinking of Uncle Henry. She hated the idea that he would have been worried about her, wondering where she'd disappeared to.

'Yes, exactly the same. The ten o'clock coach will take you to the right time. Now off to bed with you both,' chided Gerty. 'Pyjamas are three rows down.'

Alex was glad to go, not because she intended to sleep anytime soon, but because time alone would give her a chance to think. Clearly, there was no convincing Gerty to let her stay a little longer. Even Jasper was set on her returning in the morning. But just because Jasper was prepared to accept a lifetime of exile and lose his Time Passport for ever, didn't mean she was going to let him. He'd already taken huge risks and made even bigger sacrifices to be her friend. The very least she could do was try to help him.

If only she knew how.

Then there was the matter of her destiny, a secret that everybody in the world seemed to know except her. A secret that for her entire life had been whispered in a voice she couldn't quite hear. She knew now that there had been hints for as long as she could remember. The crowds of strangers that knew her name, the people who stared at her in the street and the supermarket. All those people coming to see her perform as a llama. There had always been signs. She'd just never known what they meant.

There was still something deep in the pit of her stomach that told her they'd got the wrong person. She was . . . nothing. If you'd asked her classmates and teachers at school, they'd tell you that easily enough. She wasn't going to be a popstar, or a politician, or a top lawyer. It was like Mrs Wright had said; she was Alex Nobody. Unless she wasn't. And if she really was special, then Alex wanted to get all the facts. If she knew who she was destined to be, maybe she could find a way to get there.

She needed some answers. And she needed them tonight.

*

Alex and Jasper followed Gerty's instructions to find the pyjamas. Alex changed into a floor-length Victorian nightgown and Jasper selected a silk shirt and trouser set from the 1940s. Then they searched for the toothbrushes. There were trays filled with them, from electric brushes to wooden sticks. Jasper picked up one of the sticks and started enthusiastically attacking his mouth.

'Eugh!' Alex said. 'That's someone else's toothbrush.'

'Dis schtick bewonged to Confooschiius.'

'Sorry?'

Jasper removed the stick from his mouth. 'This toothbrush belonged to a philosopher called Confucius. He lived over two thousand years ago in China.'

Alex nodded encouragingly but decided to brush her teeth with her finger. When Jasper was finished with the toothbrush, he gave another yawn, much louder than the last. 'I suppose we better get to sleep, like Gerty said.'

He turned to go, but Alex didn't move. She would try one last time. 'Jasper, I don't want to go to bed. I can't go back to my time, not without knowing why you came to watch over me in the past. Will you tell me?'

Jasper paused, a look of pain on his face. For a second, Alex thought he was going to tell her, he was just finding the right words. Then, very gently, he said, 'I can't Alex, I'm sorry. Telling you could change the future. You might not become the person you're destined to be. I wouldn't be sent back to watch over you. And we'd never have met.'

'But I've no idea who it is I'm meant to become. So how will I know if I'm taking the right path? If you give me a clue, I can make sure I'm doing the right thing.'

Jasper laughed. 'You don't need any clues. Just be yourself, that's all, and you'll get there soon enough.'

'But—'

'Do you think that if somebody told Einstein who he was going to become that he'd still have made all those amazing discoveries? Maybe, but maybe not. If you were playing a game of football and knew that, whatever you did, you were going to win, would you try as hard? Probably not. That's why you can't know, Alex.'

Alex was silenced. 'If you can't tell me, then at least come back to live with me and Uncle Henry. Murford isn't the most exciting place in the world, and school is nothing like the Time Academy, but we'd have fun. Tomorrow morning you can sneak in the luggage compartment of the coach, like I did before.'

Alex caught the look of longing in his eyes before he shook his head. 'They'd catch me before the engine started. You heard what Gerty said; all the Time Guards are out to find me. And I have a chip. It's hopeless. No; we'll try our best to get you back. And then that's the end of it.'

There was a lump in Alex's throat the size of a lemon.

'It's not hopeless,' she yelled. 'You'll see!' Alex couldn't bear to look at Jasper for another minute. She lifted her Victorian nightgown above her ankles and stormed past him, breaking into a run, to the end of the aisle, then right, and left, until she was far enough away that she could no longer hear him calling her name.

She stopped to catch her breath. As her breathing slowed, and the red mist of anger gradually lifted, she began to feel foolish. Jasper was only telling her what she already knew to be true. Tomorrow they would have to say goodbye for ever. And now, on their last evening, she had shouted at him and run away.

Alex was about to turn back to apologise to Jasper, tell him she was sorry for all the trouble she'd caused him, when her thoughts were interrupted by a loud sneeze.

She wasn't as alone as she'd thought. Somebody was standing in the shadows at the end of the passage, smiling broadly in the dim light.

CHAPTER NINETEEN
Einstein's Bicycle

Arthur Foxtail leaned against a wardrobe, inspecting his nails. 'He's wrong, you know.'

'Wrong about what?' Alex said cautiously.

'There *is* someone who could help you. Find the answers, you know.'

'You?' she asked, incredulously.

He chuckled. 'Heavens, no. Not me. I'm in enough trouble with the Time Guards already. If I told you who you become, they'd lock me up and throw away the key for ever.'

'Who, then?'

His eyes shone intensely. 'The Time Minister.'

Alex inhaled. 'Really?' she said incredulously.

'Yep. If you want to save poor Jasper from a lifetime of exile, if you want to find out who we all think you are, well, you'll need to speak to the person who controls Time Law. Go straight to the top, as they say.'

'But – but that's impossible,' she spluttered. 'The Time Minister is in Big Ben. It will be impossible to get in there with all the Time Guards around.'

Arthur slapped his knees and straightened. 'You're probably right. Never mind. Guess you'll never know. Good night.' He turned on his heel.

'No, wait!'

He paused, turning back. 'Yes?'

She took a deep breath. 'How will I get out of here without Gerty catching me? The Time Guards are one thing, but there isn't much that gets past her.'

'You're right about that,' he said, thoughtfully. 'Only an utter dingbat would try to trick Gerty.' Alex bit her lip. Arthur broke into another broad grin. 'Lucky for you, I s'pose, I'm fifty per cent dingbat. On my father's side.'

Excitement coursed through Alex's veins. Nevertheless, she hesitated. 'Why are you helping me?'

'I've known you, in a way, since you were this big –' he held his fingers inches apart – 'It's my duty to help you out.' He fiddled with his hands slyly. 'Also, I trust you'll remember this in years to come. When you're all grown up. A criminal like me could do with friends in . . . high places.'

Alex didn't understand what he meant by this. But she didn't have the luxury of questioning his motives any further. 'How will I get there? Earlier I went on a Cy-cle with Gerty, but without a chip in my brain that won't work. Walking would take ages. I don't have that kind of time.' She sighed. 'I never thought I'd miss a good old-fashioned bicycle, or a taxi.'

'Yes,' Arthur agreed. 'If only we were somewhere with old-fashioned things.'

'Do you mean there are bicycles here?'

He grinned. 'Oh, but I do. Gerty keeps transport near the back. Fancy taking a gander?'

Alex followed Arthur deep into the collection. At last she saw a glint of a shiny silver grill, and as they got closer, she realised that the silver grill was connected to an even shinier car. It was long and sleek, the colour of pink bubblegum, with a white roof. Alex brushed her fingertips along the smooth cold metal.

'Woah,' she breathed.

Arthur's fingers were locked behind his back, feet pointing in different directions. He kept some distance from her, like a car salesman hiding his eagerness for a sale. 'Belonged to Elvis, this one,' he said, casually.

'Can I?'

'Be my guest.'

Alex opened the door and slid on to the cream leather seat, enjoying the feeling of soft cushion beneath her bottom. She wrapped her fingers around the steering wheel, imagining herself gliding down an open road.

Arthur ducked his head through the open window. 'It's nice, kid, but not sure we'll have much luck getting it down the stairs without Gerty noticing.'

Alex reluctantly got out of the car.

'How about this,' he continued, nodding at a huge puff of silky blue and gold fabric. 'Took flight in Paris in 1783. It's the world's first hot air balloon to carry passengers. A sheep, a duck and a rooster, to be precise. You can't imagine the mess I found in the basket when I pinched it.'

'I don't think I know how to fly a hot air balloon.'

'Then perhaps one of these will do the job,' replied Arthur. He shepherded her beyond the cars. 'You know, bikes were always my favourite thing to steal. Probably because it was so easy. Nobody's a bit surprised when they vanish.'

Bicycles of every shape and colour were parked in a long, jumbled line. Arthur wheeled out a black and white one with large wheels. 'Try this on for size. Life is like riding a bicycle,' he said, a misty look in his eyes. 'To keep your balance, you must keep moving.'

'Woah, did you make that up?'

'No. Albert Einstein did. The owner of that bike.'

Alex took the handlebars from Arthur. She remembered what Jasper had said before about Einstein and how he might not have become who he was if he'd known his future. She walked the bike forwards a few paces. The wheels dragged a little across the floor as if they were moving through gravel. After a few turns, though, they loosened up.

'This should get me there, Arthur. But what happens when I arrive?' asked Alex. 'I'm sure there will be Time Guards watching over the Time Minister's office. How will I get past them?'

'You'll think of something,' Arthur replied. 'Now, if you'll excuse me, I need to take care of a few things to make sure Gerty doesn't get suspicious. Meet me by the stairs with the bike when you're ready to go.'

With that, Arthur disappeared into the collection, leaving Alex alone with her racing thoughts. She paced up and down. Breaking into the Time Academy that morning had worked mostly because Alex had the element of surprise. Nobody had suspected a child from the past would turn up out of the blue and no one had been prepared for an intruder missing a chip. Now that the guards knew about her, it would be far harder to get past them.

Think it through logically, she said to herself, still pacing. *What do you know about the Time Guards?* They all have chips in their brains, for one, which somehow Gerty manages to interfere with when she steals things from the past. Perhaps, thought Alex with a surge of excitement, *she* could find a way to do the same.

Ever since she was small, Alex had loved to take things apart and put them back together again. There wasn't a child in the world who knew more than her about complicated things like radio signals and electromagnetics. With the right tools and a few calculations, maybe she could build a machine to interfere with the Time Guards' brain chips. Something to distract them long enough for her to slip by. Something using technology from the past – they wouldn't be expecting that. And Alex was lucky enough to be standing in a collection full of wonderfully old objects.

To start with, Alex needed some supplies. Frowning determinedly, she set off in search of a screwdriver, hammer and glue. Next, she gathered as many electronic gadgets as she could carry – alarm clocks, radios, lamps, speakers and walkie-talkies – spreading them all out on the floor in a huge pile. Then she set to work feverishly. With the precision of a surgeon, she took out wires, coils, antenna, batteries, magnets, transistors and dials. Her tongue sticking out with concentration, she made the necessary calculations, using everything she'd learned from her uncle over the years. Then she carefully connected the parts together.

When everything was in the right place, she took a step back to admire her creation. It looked like a cross between a satellite dish and a laser gun, with two long antennae and dials of different sizes. It wasn't pretty. *But it should do the job,* she thought hopefully. It had to.

Alex looked at her watch and gasped. *How did it get so late?* She would have liked to tinker with the machine a little longer, to test it out and experiment until she could be completely sure it would work. But there was no time. Gently, she placed the machine in the bicycle's front basket and set off in the direction of the stairs.

On the way, she stopped by the wardrobe section to change back into her ordinary school uniform; even with chips in their brains, she thought someone might notice a girl cycling around in pyjamas. It was eerily quiet in the collection, and dark too. It had transformed from the place of wonder it had been in the daytime to somewhere monsters lurked in every corner. Sharp teeth, claws and glowing eyes revealed themselves to be a lawn mower, a feather hat and a pair of spoons. She hurried past as quickly as she could, trying her best to be brave. Before each corner she took a deep breath, readying herself in case Gerty waited on the other side. Deep down, she hoped Jasper would be there, even though he'd probably gone to bed. But she didn't see another soul before reaching the stairs. She arrived to a dull *thunk, thunk, thunk*.

'You took your time.' Arthur's head appeared at the top of the stairs, dragging a mannequin with a tangled clump of brown hair from the floor below. 'I'll put this in one of the beds. They'll be none the wiser if they check on you.'.

'Where are the others now?'

'Looking for Mrs Puff. She's . . . urrr . . . gone missing.' Arthur winked.

'Where is she?' Alex gasped. 'You haven't done something to her?'

'Oh, she's fine. Enjoying some leftovers in the basement. I'll bring her back up when you're gone.' There was a muffled knock. It sounded like it came from the collection, somewhere close. Arthur jumped, waving the wig at Alex urgently. 'You should get a move on.'

Alex hesitated. She'd realised a flaw in the plan. 'Arthur, how will I know the way?'

Arthur frowned. 'That's a good question. How *did* people get places before we had chips in our brains?'

'They used maps.' Alex gasped. 'Oh, *maps*!' She left the bike with Arthur and rushed back into the collection. She found the cabinet easily enough, the one she'd seen earlier with the Cleopatra scrolls. She yanked open drawers until she found what she needed. She returned moments later clutching a piece of paper.

'It's a map of London.' Arthur's face was blank, so Alex went on. 'It's like a . . . picture of the city on a piece of paper. You use it to find places. This one is quite old, but London can't have changed that much.'

'Quite old' was an understatement. It was a map of Victorian London, etched in black ink across thick yellow paper. At the centre snaked the blue line of the River Thames. Alex traced her finger along the curve of the river.

'I know London has changed a lot since this map was drawn. But there's the Houses of Parliament, look. And that's the bridge we crossed earlier.' Alex's brow was furrowed in concentration. 'When we cycled back from the Time Academy earlier, we went straight for a while, I think, then turned right. That means Gerty's place must be somewhere around here.' She tapped a spot in the bottom left of the map to show Arthur, who looked bewildered.

'If you say so . . .' Arthur said. 'My head hurts looking at that. But there you are. You'd better get going.'

'Thank you, Arthur. For helping me.'

'You can thank me later. Get on the road!'

With the map tucked under her arm, Alex manoeuvred the bike down the stairs. She tried not to make any noise, but the bike was heavy and difficult to control. It was all she could do not to let the wheels run away from her and crash straight to the bottom. As she approached the last step, she broke into a run, crossing the shop floor through an obstacle course of clothes and hangers. At the doors, she glanced quickly behind her, then opened them and stepped outside.

It was late evening now and the glare of city lights burned bright. Alex threw her leg over the bike and edged on to the road. Even for someone with a good sense of direction, finding the Time Academy by herself was going to be a challenge. Especially when her map was hundreds of years out of date. Luckily, though, Alex was the kind of person who enjoyed a challenge. She wasn't bad at map-reading, either. Uncle Henry thought it was important that she knew how to read a map – although he could hardly have predicted this kind of situation. It was one of many important life lessons he had taught her, alongside how to build a telescope from empty toilet rolls and how to make a noise *exactly* like an elephant. Neither of those lessons had proved quite as useful yet, but there was still time.

Alex spread the map across her handlebars and walked the bicycle down the street, scanning the buildings. She finally found a plaque on a boarded-up laundrette called Central Suds. It was partly obscured by dirt, but she could make out the words.

WALWORTH ROAD SE17

This was a good start. She studied the map carefully. Looking for the same road on the old map was a bit like searching for a needle in a haystack. She knew there was a chance its name had been different back in Victorian times. She traced her finger from the Houses of Parliament across and downwards.

'Aha,' she breathed. There it was, spelled out in black capital letters. On the map, Walworth Road only had a few buildings and lots of empty space. It wasn't anything like the crowded high street she found herself on now. She traced a route back to the Time Academy and was relieved to see it didn't look that far on the map. A few long, straight roads and a couple of turns. So long as Alex could get to the river, she would soon find the Time Academy.

Alex tucked the map into the bicycle's basket. Her knuckles were white on the handles. With a hard push on the pedals, she was off.

The bike wobbled at first. Alex turned the pedals faster, up and down, up and down, until she'd gathered enough momentum to move smoothly through the streets. She was cycling towards answers. She was cycling towards her destiny. Perhaps once she found out what it was, her whole life would make sense.

It was peculiar to think she would be famous, one day. Alex had never once wished for fame, unlike most children. She liked keeping herself to herself. She enjoyed reading her books and learning her facts. She was happiest when faced with a mathematical equation or tricky scientific theorem. She never wanted to be the centre of attention. Her one and only wish had been granted the day that Jasper had knocked on her door. It made her happier than fame or fortune ever could, to have a friend like him.

Flying down the street, Alex enjoyed the feeling of

the wind whipping through her hair. It wasn't long before she left the boarded-up shops and cafés behind and came to a busy main road. Alex stopped to consult the map. She was fairly sure she needed to turn right but the roads on the map didn't seem to exist any more and nearly all of the Victorian houses had been replaced by gigantic glass towers. She took a chance and turned right.

The road she turned on to was even busier than the last. Cy-cles zoomed by with a *whoosh . . . whoosh . . . whoosh*. Alex looked enviously at their riders. What she would have given to have a machine do all the hard work for her. She tried her best to keep up with the flow of traffic but the road seemed to go on for ever. Eventually, her legs started to slow and sweat gathered on her forehead. Her muscles urged her to stop. It was then she remembered what Einstein had said. *Life is like riding a bicycle. To keep your balance you must keep moving.*

She shouted the words to herself, knowing nobody else could hear her.

'You . . . just . . . need . . . to . . . keep . . . moving!'

When she finally reached the next junction, Alex took a left turn. One or two buildings along the street looked familiar to her. Nestled between two glass towers she saw a church. It looked very small and old amongst the glossy giants. There was a chance, Alex thought excitedly, that it was old enough to be on the Victorian map. She moved her finger along the map, tracing the route she hoped she was on. And yes, there it was! She let out a cry of happiness. According to the map, she was heading straight for the river.

After a while, the road started to narrow. The skyscrapers became fewer and the buildings older. She cycled past a theatre and a small park. There were more pedestrians than before and some gave her funny looks. Alex supposed her bicycle must have seemed very old-fashioned to them, a bit like seeing someone ride a penny-farthing through the streets of Murford. She careered her bike through the crowds of people. Emerging on the other side, Alex finally caught sight of water.

'The river!'

She stopped and, craning her neck, peered upwards. She could have cried to see it. Glowing against the night sky was the round face of the clock tower.

Alex pedalled as fast as she could. She raced along the curve of the river in the direction of the Time Academy. She reached the bridge in only a few minutes and turned on to it with a screech of her tyres. It was only then that she discovered there was a problem.

Standing in a line across the width of the bridge, forming a green wall of bodies, were Time Guards. Lots of them. They completely blocked Alex's path. At the centre, with a face like thunder, was the head teacher, Ms Crale.

'Stop right there.' Her calm, sharp voice travelled across the bridge. 'I knew you'd come back here. You want to know who you become, don't you? Well, you've wasted a journey. We can't tell you. We are taking you home to your own time, Alex, before you cause any more trouble.'

Alex suddenly felt very small and silly, sitting on her old rusted bike in the middle of the huge bridge. There was no way she could get past Ms Crale and so many Time Guards on a bicycle. Her mouth was dry. She knew what she had to do.

Ignoring Ms Crale, Alex parked her bike. It was time to find out whether her invention actually worked. Carefully, she picked up the machine and walked back to the centre of the bridge. Pointing the device towards the line of guards, she took a deep breath.

'I thought you were too old for toys,' said Ms Crale, scornfully. 'Come here, now. Enough of this nonsense. I've instructed the Time Guards not to let you get away this time. There won't be a repeat of earlier.'

Alex counted one . . . two . . . three . . . then she twisted one dial and another, until she heard the machine make a gentle whirring sound. Alex's eyes shot to the Time Guards, who stared right back at her. Not one of them gave the slightest indication that anything had happened. Ms Crale laughed coldly.

'I don't know what you were expecting to happen, but you've run out of options!' Her dark hair moved in the evening breeze. 'Time to hand yourself in.'

Why isn't the machine working? thought Alex. *Maybe I'm too far away and the signal can't reach them* . . . Against her better judgement, she crept towards the wall of Time Guards.

'That's it,' said Ms Crale, encouragingly. 'Come to us and we'll take you safely back to your own time. Forget about Jasper Song. He's nothing more than a criminal.'

When Alex was as close as she dared to go, she stopped and raised the machine. For the second time, she twisted the dials. The familiar whirring sound began. Only this time, the effect was immediate.

At first one, then two, and then more and more guards clutched at their heads and scrunched their eyes closed. Here and there came groans and yelps. They fell out of their neat line and scattered across the bridge.

'Can . . . you . . . hear . . . that?' shouted one guard to another, frantically turning around in a circle.

'Yes . . . !' replied another through clenched teeth. 'How . . . do . . . we . . . make . . . it . . . stop?'

Ms Crale, her own head clutched in her hands, was shouting at the guards. 'Forget . . . the . . . noise . . . and . . . apprehend her!'

Alex looked at her invention with disbelief. *It worked!* There wasn't much time to celebrate, however. For all she knew, it could stop working at any minute, so she had to get moving. Putting the device down on the ground, Alex set her sights on the clock tower.

She broke into a run, slipping straight through the chaotic crowd of Time Guards, who were still too distracted by the noise in their heads to do anything to stop her, and past the grimacing Ms Crale. Hair whipping wildly behind her, Alex came to the end of the bridge. From this distance the clock tower no longer looked like a toy, as it had earlier that day. It loomed menacingly above her head, so high she could barely see the glowing clock face. Was she really going all the way up there? She caught her breath, smoothed the hair away from her face and straightened her back. 'Yes, I am,' she said to herself, trying to sound braver than she felt.

Across the road she came to a cobbled path set between

trees. As fast as her tired legs would take her, Alex raced down the short path to the base of the clock tower. When she reached the tower's sand-coloured wall, she stopped for a few seconds to catch her breath. Then she continued along the side of the building until she came to a door.

It was an unremarkable door, made of plain wood and glass. Uncle Henry would have had to dip his head to pass through it. Written in gold letters across the front were the words CLOCK TOWER. To Alex's surprise, there was no handle, so instead she pushed. As she placed both palms on the door, the wood beneath her fingers lit up with green light.

There was a loud click and the door swung open. Alex gave a squeal of victory. She didn't know how exactly, but she had done it. She was in! Her joy was quickly followed by trepidation. This was it, she thought nervously, as she stepped inside, leaving the door slightly open in case she had to run straight out again.

Alex was standing at the bottom of a staircase. Her heart was in her throat as she looked up. Steps wound high above her head, seemingly never ending, ascending all the way to the clouds. At the top was the Time Minister.

Alex braced herself for the climb ahead. And for whatever awaited her after.

CHAPTER TWENTY

It's About Time

The climb was long. Alex clung to the black iron railing, pulling herself up and up and up and up, stopping every few floors to catch her breath. It was dizzying work. She dared not look down the middle of the staircase in case she collapsed. Under her breath, to keep herself moving, Alex counted the steps in groups of ten. One . . . two . . . three . . . four . . . five . . . *can't stop now* . . . six . . . seven . . . *just need to keep going* . . . eight . . . nine . . . ten.

Finally, she arrived at the top to find a small landing and a door. Alex rested for a minute against it. Her heartbeat refused to slow, thumping loudly in her ears. On the other side of the door, her destiny awaited. She'd broken the laws of Time Travel. She was a fugitive. And she was about to meet the most powerful person in the country. The Time Minister was sure to be angry, furious even. Alex shuddered to think what was in store for her.

But she couldn't turn back now. The answer lay behind that door.

Alex took a deep breath and opened the door. It took her a few seconds to adjust to what she saw on the other side. The walls, the ceiling, the floor, everything was painted bright white. The room was narrow; she could have touched the walls on either side with her fingers at the same time. It was very much how she'd imagined heaven to be, like a tunnel right through the clouds. Except, unlike her idea of heaven, it was remarkably cramped and smelled faintly of rust.

Alex followed the curve of the hallway, tracing her hands against the smooth white walls. Before long, the corridor opened into a small chamber. It was as narrow as before but considerably brighter and with an elevated ceiling. With a jolt, Alex realised the wall to her right had disappeared. Towering above her in its place was the pearly-white face of the clock.

This close up, the clock's delicate markings looked even more beautiful. Across the centre of its face was a criss-cross pattern she hadn't noticed before that looked like a flower. The black numerals were longer than both her arms stretched out. On the opposite wall hung hundreds of small yellow lamps, giving the clock the glow that could be seen across the city. Walking close to the opal glass – so close she could touch it – Alex wondered whether she could be seen on the other side. A small, Alex-shaped shadow looking out over London like a ghost.

She continued along the twisting corridor. Soon, she reached another clock face identical to the last, and then another and another, until she had seen all four of the tower's faces. Still, there was no sign of the Time Minister.

At the end of the corridor was yet another staircase. Alex stifled a groan; she couldn't believe the building could climb any higher. Ascending the steps, she became aware of a noise. *TING . . . TING . . . TING . . . TING . . .* Like someone hitting the side of a giant tin can with a coin.

The room she emerged into at the top of the stairs was small – with barely enough room for Alex to stand – and crammed with machinery. Giant wheels twitched clockwise; beside them smaller wheels spun more quickly in the same direction. In the middle of it all, a long pendulum swung gently backwards and forwards.

Alex was mesmerised by the pendulum's motion. Seeing the inside of this magnificent clock was comforting, almost peaceful – the rhythmic ticking sound, the constant turning of the wheels. It gave her a sense of focus, a glimmer of control after all the chaos of the last few days. She was completely at ease when she heard the voice.

'Hello.'

It seemed to come from nowhere. Hot fear surged through Alex's body. She turned frantically to see who had spoken. 'Who's there?' she asked.

The speaker laughed. It was a warm, familiar sound. 'You already know who I am.'

'Yes,' said Alex, hesitantly. She was speaking to the air. 'You're the Time Minister.'

'I am.' The voice was frail, gentle, kind. It made Alex relax, just a little. If only she knew where the voice was coming from.

'Where are you?'

'There's a ladder. Do you see it?' Alex noticed for the first time a ladder in the corner of the room. It led to a small hole in the floorboards above. 'Climb up it.'

Alex didn't move. 'I know you're scared,' said the voice, softly. 'Believe me, I do. But you're perfectly safe. I promise.' The floorboards above creaked. 'There are things you'd like to know about your past, about your future. Come upstairs and we can have a chat.'

The clock mechanism whirred. The pendulum swung. The seconds counted down with a *TING, TING, TING*. Alex walked slowly across the room and took hold of the first rung.

Reaching the top, Alex clambered to her feet. She was standing in a tiny room at what must be the highest part of the clock tower. Above her head, within the eaves of the pointed roof, hung an enormous black bell. She was surrounded by windows the shape of tombstones; none of the windows had glass and cold wind whistled through the room. At the centre, sitting in a green velvet chair behind a desk, was a very elderly woman.

'Welcome to my office. My goodness,' she said, her voice shaky with age. 'It's very good to see you at last.'

Alex stared, speechless. 'You're the Time Minister?'

The woman nodded, smiling. Her skin was tremendously wrinkly, like a blouse that had been tumble-dried for hours and hours. In the soft light, Alex couldn't tell whether it was emotion or the wind that caused her eyes to water. She had wisps of white hair, like marshmallow, half pulled up on to her head, half hanging to her shoulders.

'Do you live up here?'

'Heavens, no. This is where I work. The whirring of the mechanisms helps me think. And the fresh air rushing through the windows. The stairs are a challenge, but they keep me fit.'

Alex studied the old woman's face curiously. Despite her years, it was bright and strong. Her back was curved over, as often happens with age. Still, she managed to sit up in the chair with impressive dignity.

'I'm not what you were expecting,' she said, her eyes twinkling.

'No, no,' said Alex hastily. 'It's just . . .'

'Yes?'

'No, you aren't what I was expecting,' admitted Alex, shyly. She wasn't sure exactly what she had expected, but it was certainly not this. 'It's not only that though. It sounds strange but I feel like I know you. Like we've met before. That's not possible . . . is it?'

The woman said nothing, her lips pressed tightly together. Alex struggled to process her thoughts. She recognised the old woman, not merely as a familiar face, but as if she had known her for her entire life. Alex remembered pictures that Uncle Henry had shown her a long time ago. Of a woman with eyes like her own and a kind smile.

'Are you . . . are you . . .' She swallowed, building up the courage to ask the question. 'Are you my mother?'

The old woman's glazed with sadness. Slowly, she shook her head.

Alex nodded, hiding her disappointment. 'I don't understand.'

'I'm afraid to say that, even at my age, there's not much I understand. In fact, sometimes I think that life only becomes less clear as you get older. You start off with all the answers and gradually, second by second, year by year, one by one, you forget them.'

The old woman stared beyond Alex and up at the great bell hanging above their heads. Alex wondered nervously what would happen if it chimed; surely, this close, it would be deafening. Neither of them made a sound for several seconds, listening only to the ticking pendulum below.

The Time Minister was the one to finally break the silence. 'Look at me again. Really look. Have you worked out why you know me? Come, come. Come closer.'

Alex took a deep breath. Cautiously, she closed the distance between them. She looked hard at the elderly woman's face, searching her brain for a memory, a clue as to why she felt so familiar. Nothing. The old woman's eyes met hers; despite her frailty they were fierce, determined. And suddenly, with a sense of shock, Alex realised that she *did* know.

She stumbled backwards. 'No! You can't be ... I can't be.'

Slowly, and with what looked like great effort, the Time Minister rose to her feet. She leaned her hands on the desk. Watching Alex carefully, she said, 'It must come as a great shock. In fact, I know very well how you are feeling. How difficult it is to understand. But it's true. We are one and the same, you and I. That's why your fingerprints opened the door to my office.'

'But ... but ... you can't be. You're the Time Minister!'

Wind whooshed through the room, rustling the old woman's white hair. Alex shook with disbelief. She thought her knees might collapse beneath her. She couldn't process what she was being told, yet she knew in her heart it was true. 'You ... you're me?'

'Yes. And I'm you.'

Alex was numb. She touched her own face, her nose, her cheeks. She looked at the wrinkled skin of the elderly woman sitting before her. The old woman's nose was larger and longer than her own; her eyes sunk within layers of crumpled skin. Etched across her forehead were deep lines and sunspots. Alex had never imagined herself old. She'd always thought, deep down, that things would stay the same for ever – that *she* would stay the same for ever. She'd half-thought that old people had always been old, as if they had arrived on the planet that way, ready formed with a cane and false teeth. How could she become the old lady standing in front of her? How could her face become so different? And yet, the old woman's eyes, her large brown eyes, were unmistakably her own.

'If it's true that you are me . . .' Alex choked on the words; they seemed so incredible. 'Then why? Why did you bring me here?'

The old lady smiled. 'You came looking for *me*, if I remember rightly.'

'I came looking for my friend.'

'Yes,' the Time Minister sunk into her chair. 'I remember that too.'

Alex trembled. Ever since that rainy afternoon in the alleyway when Jasper had told her that he'd been sent to Murford to watch over her, she had wondered who she would become. Now that she was staring into the eyes of her future, it was suddenly real. She knew exactly who she was going to become. And yet she had more questions than ever.

'How did you – how did I – become the Time Minister? Gerty said that you'd discovered how to travel in t—'

'Oh, Gerty!' The Time Minister's dark eyes shone brilliantly. 'I do miss my old friend. How is she? Still breaking rules like they don't apply to her?'

Alex stammered words like *how* and *what* and *but*, trying to order her thoughts into a sentence. When she gave up, the Time Minister began again.

'I appointed Gerty as a professor of the Time Academy many years ago. She was a wonderful teacher and the students loved her. But I knew that eventually I would have to dismiss her. Or she wouldn't start her collection – her way of getting back at me, I presume. And then, you see, she wouldn't have been at the coach station to bump into you yesterday morning.' She sighed. 'Of course, it made me miserable to send her away like that. I'm sure she thinks I'm wicked for it. But I'm afraid it was how it had to be.'

'But wh—'

'Don't ask me why,' the Time Minister said. 'I might understand the physics of time, the beautiful, remarkable mechanics of it. But the bigger questions . . .

about why things happen and when? I haven't the foggiest.'

'How did you do it?' Alex asked. 'How did you discover a way to travel in time?'

'I'm an old lady,' the Time Minister replied, laughing. 'I can't remember what I had for lunch yesterday. And you expect me to remember that?' Alex began to protest, and the Time Minister held up a hand.

'You'll figure out the answer to that question in the same way I did. Largely by accident and after a lot of hard work. Not a moment sooner.'

It was finally starting to sink in. Everything strange and unexplained that had ever happened to Alex since the day she was born was because of who she was destined to become. 'That's why all those people came to watch me in school plays, science fairs and things,' she said slowly. 'They were coming to see you – or me, except I didn't know it yet. But what about Jasper? Why did you send him to watch over me?'

The Time Minister looked dreamily at her hands and sighed. 'Never underestimate the power of a best friend. A friend who loves you for who you are, who believes in the person you will become even when you don't. Who believes you are stronger, smarter, better than you believe yourself to be. A friend who can put you in your place when you need it. More than talent, more than success, friendship is what matters most. If you want to know how I did it, how I discovered the secrets of time, you only need to understand that.'

The Time Minister breathed heavily, as if each inhale was a great effort. Jasper's face appeared vividly in Alex's mind, his hopeful expression on the night he'd shown up on her doorstep. She thought about the way they could talk about anything and would always end up laughing. About how much he'd been willing to sacrifice for her. What would happen to him now?

'Speaking of friendship, I believe our guest is about to arrive.' The Time Minister craned her neck towards the hole in the floor. 'If my memory serves me correctly, which it so rarely does these days.'

Alex tensed. As the Time Minister had predicted, there was movement below. Then the ladder creaked, rung by rung. Moments later, a head of dark, sticky-up hair rose through the gap in the floorboards.

Jasper scrambled to his feet. His face was covered in sweat and he was breathing hard. Alex thought it looked like he'd sprinted the whole way up the tower.

'Your Excellency,' he spluttered. 'Please . . . please . . .'

He was unable to continue, gulping down air like a fish out of water. 'Excuse the intrusion, your Excellency,' he managed, after taking a minute to catch his breath. 'The door was open so I let myself in. I'm sorry that I failed my mission. I broke Time Law and I'm here to receive my punishment. But first, please, let me escort Alex on to a coach back home to Murford. Let me fix my mistake, your Excellency.'

Alex stared open-mouthed at Jasper. She didn't notice that the Time Minister had gotten up until she hobbled – with remarkable speed for her age – halfway across the room. With a sun-spotted hand, she gently touched Jasper's cheek. 'Hello, Jasper. My old friend. How glad I am to see you.'

Jasper, obviously startled, quickly lowered himself into a bow.

'No! Stop, stop,' the Time Minister said, crossly. 'None of that.'

Jasper's eyes widened and he talked fast. 'Whatever punishment you think I deserve, your Excellency, I'm ready for it.'

'There will not,' the Time Minister said, firmly, 'be any punishment.'

'But I failed—'

'You haven't failed at anything, Jasper. You've done

fantastically, as I knew you would. You broke the rules to be there for a friend who needed you. You were kind, brave and selfless. That's mission accomplished, if you ask me.'

Jasper looked sideways at Alex, bewildered. 'But Ms Crale . . . and Mr Parrot . . .'

'Try not to judge them too harshly, Jasper. Your head teacher couldn't understand why I would send a boy like you on such an important mission. I tried to explain to Selena Crale that there are more important things than good marks. Like imagination, passion, loyalty. She knew all those things once – all children do – but with time has forgotten. It's remarkably easy to forget, when you become powerful, and old, what it's like to be young, curious, uncertain about the world. Since you joined the school, Jasper, you've reminded me of that. I can't thank you enough.' The Time Minister beamed up at him, a little wobbly on her feet. 'Now, would you kindly help an old lady back to her chair?'

Jasper did as he was told, taking her by the arm to the desk. Once she was settled, he let the air out of his lungs slowly. His face was flushed with shock and relief, like he had found a winning lottery ticket in his trouser pocket, seconds before throwing them in the washing machine. He looked back and forth between Alex and the Time Minister. 'So now you know about your future.'

'Not everything. There's lots I don't,' Alex replied. She turned to the Time Minister. 'Now that I know, won't it all change? Couldn't I do things differently and not end up discovering Time Travel after all? Jasper said that might happen if he told me about . . . about my future.'

'Remember what I said about friendship?' the Time Minister said with a yawn. 'So long as you remember that, everything else will take care of itself.'

Alex wasn't entirely satisfied with this answer. But the old woman's eyelids were drooping, and Alex didn't feel like she could press her any further.

'What do we do now?' Jasper whispered to Alex.

'Well, I wouldn't recommend staying here much longer,' cut in the Time Minister, opening one eye. 'Judging by the time,' she looked at her watch, 'a very large bell is about to ring. And I only have one pair of headphones.'

Alex suddenly noticed a humungous pair of ear-mufflers sitting on the desk. The old woman picked them up.

'We're free to go?' asked Jasper.

The old woman stared at him. 'I'm not about to imprison myself, now am I? Or my best friend, for that matter.'

Jasper started to say something, then stopped himself. 'What is it?' asked the Time Minister.

'There's something I'd like to ask you, but I'm afraid you'll say no.'

'Go on.'

'It's just, I *really* don't want to go back to the Time Academy,' Jasper said, the words spilling out of him. 'I've never fitted in there. And if I'm honest, I don't want to be a Time Guard. No offence. I wondered . . . I wanted to ask . . . whether I could return with Alex to Murford? It's the only place I've ever felt that I could be myself.'

The Time Minister turned towards Alex. Happiness shone in her tired eyes. 'What do you think, Alex? In a way, you're the Time Minister too. Shall we let him go with you?'

'Yes, yes, oh please, yes!'

'In that case,' the Time Minister said, with another yawn, 'I wouldn't have it any other way. Oh, I almost forgot!' She opened a drawer in her desk, rummaged around and took something out. 'You'll be needing this soon. Give me your hand.' Alex held open her palm and the Time Minister gave her something wrapped in green cloth. 'And I have a message I'd like you to pass on to Gerty for me.' The Time Minister passed her a folded note. 'Now, I missed my afternoon nap today, so if you'll both excuse me . . .'

The old woman closed her eyes, sighed contentedly, and, with a smile on her lips, fell into a deep sleep.

CHAPTER TWENTY-ONE

Back in Time for Tea

Jasper was first to reach the bottom of the clock tower. Close behind, and panting as hard, was Alex. It was approaching midnight and the sky was black and starless. They found Gerty and Arthur at the gates, bickering loudly. Both were so engrossed in their argument that they didn't look up for several seconds.

'Didn't fancy the stairs?' Alex grinned and the pair stopped arguing instantly.

'You're OK!' Gerty shrieked, face ashen, charging at them with her arms open. Then, suddenly, with a look of horror, she stepped back and dipped her head into a low bow. 'Please accept my apologies, kiddo. I mean, er, your Excellency. I made Arthur tell me on the way here about who you are . . . who you become! Of course, I had started to have my suspicions, but I tried not to think about it. I thought it best that I didn't know who you become in the future, in case it complicated things, or in case I didn't like what I discovered. She's just a kid, I told myself. A kid who needs my help.'

'Didn't you recognise me?' asked Alex.

'No, I've never seen you this young before. I made it a firm rule to never steal anything from the Time Minister herself. I was far too scared of getting caught. What if you realised your stuff was going missing and figured out what I was up to? Arthur is a little less worried about taking such risks, which is why he realised who you are a bit quicker than me. My apologies again, your Excellency.'

'You really don't need to bow,' Alex groaned.

'And this one thought he could trick me . . . *me*!' Gerty thumped Arthur hard on the arm. 'But I suppose now I understand why. I still can't believe the stowaway I agreed to harbour was none other than a young Time Minister! Never in my wildest dreams would I expect to bump into somebody like *you* in the coach station. I should have known that only somebody as brilliant as you would find a way here.'

Arthur shrugged. 'In my defence, I couldn't pass up the opportunity to get in the good books of the future

Time Minister.' Curled up in his arms was a disgruntled-looking Mrs Puff. She was clearly feeling sour at having been locked up in the basement. Even so, when Alex stroked under her chin she purred appreciatively.

Alex laughed. 'Don't be silly, Gerty. I'm still just me. Nothing has changed, not really.' And it was true. Alex felt exactly the same as before. She never thought she'd be so excited to return to Murford, to return to being a nobody.

Gerty raised an eyebrow. 'So, what did the Time Minister say? Or, I suppose, the question is; what did *you* say. Future you, that is. Or present you? Oh, this is confusing. You know what I mean.' She sighed deeply. 'I understand now why travelling to the future is against the law. It would be chaos!'

'She's letting us go back to Murford,' replied Alex. 'Both of us.'

'She is? You are? Jasper, you must be the first person in history to emigrate to another time permanently. The Time Minister must think a lot of you.'

At this, Jasper grinned. Arthur dabbed at the corners of his eyes. 'Going back together. That's beautiful, that is.' Overcome by emotion he reached over and clobbered Gerty into a hug.

Mrs Puff hissed at being pressed between them.

Gerty quickly wrestled Arthur off. 'Get . . . off . . . me . . . you great big baby! You know I don't do hugs.'

Alex laughed. Then she noticed that Jasper looked worried.

'We forgot to ask her how we'd get home,' he said.

Alex opened her fingers and revealed the small package wrapped in cloth. 'I think the Time Minister had a plan for that. I don't know what this is, but she gave me this as we were leaving.'

'A Time Crystal!' gasped Gerty, leaning in for a better look as Alex carefully removed the cloth. 'I've never seen one in real life before. They're very rare. Only a small quantity exist in the world. Incredibly valuable too.' She looked at it hungrily.

Alex closed her fingers around the crystal, drawing it away from Gerty's reach.

'Ms Crale has one,' Jasper said. 'That's how she took me back, that afternoon in the alleyway. You have to spin it very fast and it'll take you through time.'

'How far back you go depends on the speed you spin the crystal,' elaborated Gerty. 'If you get the spin just right, you'll travel back to the exact moment you travelled forwards in time. On this very spot.'

'It won't take us to Murford?'

Gerty snorted. 'Heavens, no. The crystals can only

be used to travel in time, not to travel across distances. You'll need to do that bit the old-fashioned way.'

They all fell silent, and Alex knew it was time to go. 'I suppose this isn't really goodbye, is it? More like a "see you later".'

'Whatever you call it, I'm sad to see you go.' Gerty's eyes were red at the corners and her lips quivered. 'It's been fun, kiddo.'

'Thanks for all your help. I'll never forget it.' And Alex knew quite certainly that she wouldn't.

'Wait!' Gerty exclaimed. 'You've forgotten your end of the bargain. Don't you remember what you offered me in the station? In exchange for my help.'

'Oh!' Alex took off her watch and handed it to Gerty.

Gerty put the watch on and beamed. 'I was planning to sell it, of course, but I won't now. It will be a nice souvenir to remember you by. Now, get out of here you two.'

'One more thing, Gerty.' Alex tried her best to sound matter-of-fact. She had a strange feeling that she knew what the note said. 'The Time Minister asked me to pass you this.'

Alex handed her the folded piece of paper. Gerty seemed to read it over three times before saying a word.

'There's a post opening up for a new head teacher. And . . . and . . . the Time Minister wants to offer it to me! Oh, thank you, kiddo, thank you!'

'I'll be seeing you both soon.' Alex smiled at Gerty, and then at Arthur.

Jasper held out the crystal in his palm. 'Are you ready?'

Alex nodded, and Gerty and Arthur stood back. Jasper spun the crystal in the palm of his hand and it began to whirl faster and faster, until it was nothing more than a blur of bright white light, forming a tunnel before them.

'Hold my hand!' shouted Jasper over the noise. 'In three . . . two . . . one . . .'

They walked together into the tunnel and disappeared into the darkness.

*

It was a grey morning in London, just before eleven. Birds chirped hopefully and a breeze swept through the trees. The streets were thick with tourists, who looked at the city through camera phones. Above, the minute hand of Big Ben twitched towards the hour. Nobody noticed a boy and a girl, holding hands, appear out of nowhere.

It was horribly jarring to be so suddenly in daylight, even if it was drizzling. Seconds before, Alex and Jasper had been standing under a starless sky in the middle of the night. The quick transition made Alex feel slightly sick and strange, like she'd been on a long car journey.

The pair looked at each other and smiled. Given their surroundings, they certainly seemed to be in the right time period. The crystal had worked. But they still had to get back to Murford and Alex knew they had to time it just right. Otherwise Uncle Henry would be worried.

Quickly, they set out to find a bus. When they found the right one, Alex had enough money for two tickets and a packet of crisps. They climbed on to the bus, both woozy with tiredness, having not slept since the night before, wolfed down the crisps, and fell immediately asleep.

*

'Wake up,' said Jasper. 'It's our stop!'

Alex woke with a start. She looked outside. Murford High Street, with its colourful shop windows and over-flowing dustbins, was the most welcome sight she had ever seen.

'We're home!'

They flew down the bus steps two at a time. Alex led the way, running through the streets of the town all the way to her road. She slowed only as they approached the front door, suddenly feeling nervous. Quietly, she opened it and tiptoed down the hallway to the living room. Sitting on the sofa, typing away at his laptop keyboard, was Uncle Henry. For a while, Alex stared happily at his face, his round, familiar, lovely face. Then he glanced up and noticed her.

'Oh, hello dear.' He smiled warmly, sitting up in his chair. 'You're back early. How was the science fair? Did Robo-Chick behave herself? I do hope—'

Alex flung herself at him. 'Uncle Henry,' she said, her face buried in his shoulder, 'I've missed you so much.'

Uncle Henry laughed and straightened his glasses, which had almost been knocked off his nose by the impact. 'What's all this about? Not that I didn't miss you too. 'But you've only been gone for –' he checked his watch – 'about four hours.'

'Is that all?' Alex laughed. They had timed it perfectly. 'I'm just glad to be home.'

Jasper shuffled his feet in the doorway, catching Uncle Henry's attention. 'Jasper my boy, you're here!'

he said. 'I knew you'd turn up eventually. Didn't I say, Alex, that everything would be OK?'

'Sorry to worry you,' said Jasper. He looked up at the ceiling and Alex could tell he was inventing a plausible explanation for his disappearance. She watched him carefully, unsure what he was going to say. 'I had to go away for a while. My . . . er . . . parents decided to move back to Scotland.'

'Back to Scotland?' replied Uncle Henry.

'Yes . . . but then I told them how much I like Murford. And they said that, if I really preferred it, I could come back and live with you. If that's all right, I mean.' Now Jasper was staring at the floor, his face shining with embarrassment.

Alex interrupted. 'Jasper hasn't anywhere else to stay, Uncle Henry. Can he come and live with us? Please say yes. Please!'

Uncle Henry blinked several times. 'Are you sure your parents are OK with that, Jasper?'

'Yes. But only if it's not too much trouble.'

'Too much trouble! I've always thought it was a bit quiet around here, just the two of us. I'll need to speak to your parents on the phone first,' he said, thoughtfully. 'As soon as your mother's phone is back up and running that is. But as far as I'm concerned, you're welcome to stay as long as you'd like. Now, who would like some tea? And perhaps a pickled egg or two?'

The next day, Alex had a lot of explaining to do at school. Mrs Wright was furious that she'd left in the middle of the morning without telling a soul and had not returned until the following day. Jasper, meanwhile, who'd spent *two* unexplained days away from school, was welcomed back with open, lavender-scented arms. As punishment, Alex received a seemingly endless sentence of detention. Jasper, on the other hand, was offered extra dessert at lunchtime indefinitely. However, he said he would serve detention alongside Alex, and even though their head teacher protested, he was eventually allowed.

*

Five weeks later, in a warm classroom that smelled faintly of glue, Alex was settling down to another page of maths equations in detention. Jasper, at the next desk, had his nose buried in a dusty old classic so thick it could stop a door. At the front of the room, snoring gently, their maths teacher dozed on a stack of unmarked workbooks.

That afternoon, they saw the occasional sun hat or nose poke above the classroom's window frame. These days, when strange people turned up in Alex's life like this – Time Tourists, as she now knew them to be – she either ignored them completely, or smiled and waved, depending on her mood.

Mostly, though, Alex kept her head firmly in the present. She tried not to think about the future, which became easier as time went on. Alex was far too happy with how things were right now to worry about what came next. And she had stopped thinking of herself as Alex Nobody. Not because of her grand destiny, though admittedly that helped. But because it was hard to feel like a *nobody* when she had found *somebody* so special to call a friend.

'Parallel universes. What do you reckon?' whispered Alex, looking up from her notes. 'I read in one of Uncle Henry's books last night that scientists think there could be loads of universes like our own out there, each one slightly different.'

Jasper put his book down and frowned. 'Parallel universes? Would that mean more than one Mrs Wright? If so, then I definitely hope it isn't true.'

Alex laughed. 'OK, your question next.'

Jasper thought for a moment and smiled. 'Would

you rather eat all the insects in the world . . . or kiss all the hippopotamuses?'

They both collapsed in fits of laughter. The teacher woke up with a loud snort and shouted at them for talking. Alex turned over another page of advanced equations, still smiling, and got back to work.

ACKNOWLEDGEMENTS

I have to start by thanking my parents. No, really I do, or my Mum might throw this book at me. I'm only kidding . . .

Aside from the book throwing, my parents, Chris and Robin, are the kindest people in the world. They've always made me feel I could do anything I put my mind to and at the same time provided ample inspiration for larger than life characters. They read the chapters of this book enthusiastically, one by one, as I wrote them. Without their support, and their asking 'what happens next?', I wouldn't have had the conviction to write on. For this, and for everything, I will always be grateful.

Thank you to Joanne Smith. We've always been a great creative team, right from our Barbie playing days (you designed their clothes and I made up their life stories). Thank you to Cerys Quinn, for her boundless enthusiasm and for giving me her insights as a real-life eleven-year-old, to Gillian Quinn, for reading early drafts and for always being so supportive, and to Gary Wong for generously reading the book in its early stages. Thanks also go to the rest of my family, the Quinlans, the Smiths and the Tylers, and to fellow booklover (and Sudoku master) Cheryl Sims.

Thank you to Andrew Budge. You made me take myself seriously as a writer, which helped to turn a daydream about time travel into an actual book. You encouraged me when I felt like giving up, pushing me along the rollercoaster of doubt and belief that comes with writing a book. My thanks also go to the Budge family, for their endless kindness and support.

Thank you to my wonderful friends, for their belief and cheerleading, and to my colleagues who have shared in my excitement at every step in this amazing process. This includes making frenzied laps of the office when exciting news came in.

Speaking of exciting news, I am hugely grateful to my unstoppable agent Chloe Seager at Madeline Milburn Literary Agency, who took a chance on this story and makes the seemingly impossible happen.

Thank you to my brilliant editor Lena McCauley. I'm so lucky to get to work with you, and to benefit from your insight, judgement and humour. Special thanks to copy editor Genevieve Herr and proof-reader Emily Hibbs for their incredible work to make the book the best it can be, to Michelle Brackenborough and Thy Bui for the beautiful cover and design, and to marketer James McParland and publicist Lucy Clayton and the whole rest of the team at Hachette.

Finally, I would like to thank all my amazing teachers, who encouraged me to be curious, to love learning and to discover the joy in reading and writing. And I would like to thank YOU, the reader. I can't wait to hear about your own astonishing futures.

KATE GILBY SMITH

was born on the sunny island of Guernsey.
It was daydreaming during a philosophy of
time travel seminar at Edinburgh University
that she first had the idea for this story.
She now works as a publicist of science,
philosophy and history books at a
London publisher.

 @kate_gilby